The
BILLIONAIRE'S
SON

CAM KASSOM

K. RENEE

The Billionaire's Son

CAM KASSOM

K. RENEE

K. RENEE PUBLICATIONS

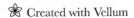 Created with Vellum

Note From the Author

Thank you all for supporting everything I do. This exclusive release was important to me and I'm so grateful that you all were acceptive of it. I wanted to also, give a little trigger warning because there is a scene in this book that involves a very small section of child abuse. I know you all hate to see this family go, but it's time that we move on and create new memories with new characters.

Love you all to life!

K. Renee

Synopsis

Cam Kassom didn't need to worry about grades. He was the best football player at LSU, with his sights set on going all the way to the league. First, he would need a tutor to keep his dreams intact. What he wasn't expecting was the annoying, kinky haired nerd assigned to be his tutor. Remi was a thorn in his side, and all he wanted was to get his grades up and be done with her. Cam had a long list of things, and women, he would rather be spending his time on, but he was forced to be in close proximity to Remi.

Remi's head was in the books and not on the frivolous college life. The last thing she wanted to be bothered with was a jock, who made a joke of his education, and just wanting to ride easy street. People who had things handed to them and didn't know the meaning of true hard work grated on her last nerve. However, tutoring was her job, and Cam needed assistance with getting his grades up to par. The last thing on Remi's mind was getting to know LSU's big man on campus. But being in close proximity to Cam did things to her hormones that she desperately wanted to ignore. It didn't matter, though… Remi had hard choices of her own that ultimately derailed her from her goals. And Cam Kassom turned out to be the least of her worries.

Both Cam and Remi led lives that ran parallel and their paths should have never crossed. However, whether they liked it or not, their connection was fated, and so was the drama that buzzed around them. Chance encounters, snakes in the grass, and tight kept secrets takes both of them on a ride neither expected.

Chapter One

CAM

I'm in my sophomore year here at LSU and things were definitely looking up for me this year. My freshman year, a nigga didn't do so good academically or anything else. I was on some other shit and showed my damn ass for the most part. That shit almost cost me my future. Athletically, I've been on fire since high school and every time you turn on the radio or Sports Center, you're bound to hear something about Cam Kassom.

I'm a big deal, especially now being that everyone is trying to figure out if I'm going into the draft this year. That life changing decision is my mom's to make, and she's taking her sweet time making it. I don't do shit without her approval, but the relationship with my dad is another story. Even though I act up a little, I'm still humble about my success. I try not to let that shit go to my head because I don't want to come off conceited or think I'm better than the next person. I treat everyone with respect, just as long as they show me the same gratitude. I'm not one of those rich bratty ass kids. I hung out with my Uncle Zelan and my Grandma Lai, so I can get down with the best of them. With that being said, it's always suggested not to try my fuckin' gangsta. The only thing I let go to my head a little are these damn females. They be ready to risk it all for a nigga, and that be having my ass on cloud nine. Even though my good outweighs the bad, there are still some out here talkin' that "I only made it this far because of my dad and his money" shit. I built my success, not my family. I'll always be grateful that they support me through it all, and that shit means the world to me. But know when I step out on that field, it's just me and God.

I'll never let muthafuckas that don't know me outside of sucking my dick or wishing they were me make is seem like privilege got me here. Fuck that! I worked my ass off, on the field and off. I hired a tutor to help me academically to ensure my athletic career was solid, so fuck these niggas that thought otherwise. I'm not dumb by far, but when God was passing out them smart ass genes to the Kassom kids, he gave all that shit to my brother JuJu. When we realized I was failing, I tried getting help from him so that I could improve in those problem areas, but I quickly told my dad to fire his ass.

The way that nigga set up an app for us to work together, it was as if we were in the same fucking room. Shit was too high-tech for my liking. The nigga had me looking around my apartment to make sure his ass wasn't really there. I told my dad I needed normalcy. JuJu's ass just wasn't it for me.

My doorbell sounded off, jolting me from my thoughts, prompting me to jump up to see who was at my door. Looking through the peephole, I saw that it was my tutor. As soon as I opened the door, she came rushing in.

"Cam! I need to shower before we get started on our study

session!" she yelled out as she ran down the hall with all this damn yellow shit all over her. I can't even imagine what this crazy ass girl had gotten herself into. Her nerdy ass was probably trying to build a volcano, and the shit erupted all over her ass. I met Remi when I was in search of a tutor. We kind of hit it off, and from that moment on, she's been my hired help ever since.

Remi wasn't the type of girl that I'm attracted to, but she was cool, and we've built a lil bond. She's smart, so I needed her in my damn corner with all these damn exams and having to keep my grades up. Playing ball is all I ever want to do, so I'm gone always take my education seriously. As serious as I took the shit though, some of this damn work just didn't click. That's where she came in and simplified it so that I could understand. Remi was a geek through and through, and although nothing is wrong with that, baby girl had the nerve to dress like one. Remi was a geek through and through, and nothing is wrong with that, but baby girl even dressed like one. She wore these thick ass circle glasses, her hair was always in a tight ass bun making her head look bigger than what it was, and her clothes always consisted of tights, sweats, and oversized t-shirts. Nothing was sexy about her wardrobe. Don't get me wrong, Urkel had potential. She could be a beautiful girl if she fixed herself up. Hell, I even offered to take her shopping and give her a makeover, but she refused my help. Name a woman that turns down a chance to spend the next man's money? Nobody but square ass Remi. I'd even advised her to get contacts because behind those thick ass bifocals, were a set of gorgeous gray eyes that reminded me of my mom's.

Just when I was about to go make sure her ass hadn't drowned in the shower since it had been well over thirty minutes. She came walking out with a towel wrapped around her body, and her wet curly hair cascaded down past her shoulders. This

5

was the first time I'd ever seen her like this. Something was different about her. With those big ass glasses off, there was a sparkle in her eye that I've never seen. Hell, her smile was even different. As if them bitches was glued to her face, I've never seen her with her glasses off or even her hair down. Her head was still kinda big though, but that made sense with the big ass brain she was sheltering. JuJu's was the same way.

"Cam, I'm so sorry I rushed in like this. Thank God I had some changing clothes in my duffle bag. I came here to clean up because your place was the closest. I hope you don't mind." She looked as if she had been crying.

"What happened to you?" I asked, as I watched her scan the room for the duffle bag she dropped while barging in.

"Your friend Saniya and her stupid friends said it was an accident, but they spilled something on the floor. I slid in it and hit the ground, getting it all in my hair and on my clothes. No matter what she said, I know it wasn't an accident, because she doesn't like me. She always has something smart to say to me or about me. To be honest, I think it has everything to do with you. I know she likes you, and she's probably mad that I'm always here with you and hanging out with you. Seriously, you need to talk to her and let her know that we have nothing going on. You don't even look at me like that. I know I'm not the type of girl you would go after." She sighed, grabbing her duffle bag and plopped down on the couch.

"Nah, that shit doesn't have anything to do with me. If it wasn't an accident, that's fucked up, and I'm gone talk to her about that shit. You know ion play about you. I can't have shit happening to my Lil Webster's Dictionary. Oh yeah, as for your last comment, you don't know what I'm into, lil baby." I winked at her, standing up from the couch, and walked into the kitchen to grab some menus to order some dinner. I mean, it's true, I'm not into her like that, but it was something about the way she said that shit that made me feel bad.

"What do you have a taste for, Remi? We can do pizza, burgers, Chinese, or chicken." She stood from the couch, and the moment I looked up, she dropped her towel. Like what the fuck wrong with this girl. She slipped and fell in that shit, and bumped her fuckin' head.

"Tell me again what you're into since I don't know." The boldness in her voice had me looking around the damn room like another chick had entered the building and was speaking on her damn behalf 'cause who the hell she thought she was coming at like that. I will fuck new life into her ass and make her forget who she was thirty minutes ago. Her best option was to pull her towel back up and find something safe to do like open my history book. I'm a damn Kassom; and I slang dick like one.

"Soo, you just gone drop yo' shit in front of me like that and think I'm not gone react?" I asked, never taking my eyes off of her.

"Yeah, because I know you're full of it! I don't have anything that you like. I barely have an ass and my breasts are non-existent. You want a girl like Saniya. She has the ass, the breasts, the hips, and she's beautiful." She shrugged, stepping closer to me and attempting to put her clothes on. The fuck she thought this was.

I let out a chuckle 'cause I know this girl ain't in here fuckin' with me! Putting pussy in my face is something her ass should never do.

"Why you in my shit playing in my face, Remi?" The look on her face was something I'd never seen before. Like was she really coming for me?

"What's wrong, Cam? You don't like what you see?" She smiled, and I think I just got my answer. Baby girl was coming for me.

"Lil baby, I'm not trying to get you caught up in some shit you can't get out of. I'm a Kassom and I slang dick like one. Trust me, I'm not it for you, baby girl. I'm damn sure not trying to hurt you or make shit weird between us," I explained as I sat on the couch, still never breaking my stare from her. I couldn't believe she was in front of me like that. She was right; she didn't have much of an ass, and her titties were the size of a damn plum. There wasn't much to hold onto, but if she kept standing in front of me like that, I'ma figure some shit out and tear her ass up.

"Fuck!" I sighed, rubbing my hands over my face. Instead of her putting some damn clothes on, this girl moved in front of me with her pussy damn near in my face. I shook my head because I knew before the night was over, I was gone break her ass in two.

"What's wrong?" she smirked. I tried to get up, but she pushed me back on the couch, straddling my lap, and my dumb ass let her. I swear the smell of pussy will have a nigga make some bad decisions. I knew if I took it there with this girl, shit might be different for us regarding our friendship.

"You're so fine, Cam," she moaned, placing small sensual kisses on my lips. For a minute, I didn't move because I couldn't believe shit was about to pop off with us. I knew better than to take it this far, but like I said pussy was my second language. She moved her hands between my legs, waking my nigga up, and that was that on that.

Lifting her into my arms, I headed into my bedroom. As soon as I placed her on the bed, I began kissing and sucking on her bottom lip. Our kiss was so intense that shit had me feeling some shit I've never in my life felt before. I wanted to be inside of her, and nothing was going to stop me. Pulling my clothes off quickly, I hovered over her, placing kisses on her lips. I moved down to her chest, latching onto her breast and caused her breathing to elevate. She started to shake uncontrollably when my fingers began massaging her pussy.

"You good?" I looked down at her. She nodded that she was alright, but I could see the nervousness in her eyes. The boldness she had in my living room was gone. Baby girl seemed as if she was about ten seconds from becoming a new track star and running the fuck up out of this room.

"Please," she whispered, pulling me close to her. I leaned over and gave her what she wanted. Spreading her legs apart, I slid my dick up and down her slit. Baby girl was shaking so bad I thought her ass was having a seizure. I eased inside of her, and she started screaming for dear life, but the part that got me was trying to get inside her was hard as fuck. Almost as if she was a virg... Fuck! I know damn well this girl ain't no...

"Remi, please tell me you're not a virgin?" I already knew what it was, and I didn't want to be the one to take a girl's virginity. Remi would be the first girl that I've been with that was a virgin. I've always heard that once you take their virginity, they get a little clingy, and I ain't trying to have that shit at all.

"Yes, and I want you to be my first. I trust you, Cam. I'm tired of being the nerdy girl around campus that's still a virgin. It will only be just sex. I promise you nothing will come back on you from this. After it's all said and done, we can act as if it never happened." She looked up at me, and I knew I should have rolled over and put my damn clothes back on. But noooo, the pussy was talking and I was listening. Leaning back in, I wrapped my lips around hers and taking my time entering her.

9

"Cam!" she cried out as I pushed inside of her. I was trying to slow my pace allowing her to adjust to my size, but that shit was extremely hard. The pussy was so tight and felt so fuckin' good.

"Fuck!" I gritted as I started to slowly move inside of her.

"Cammm! I can't... I can't take it!" she cried out. The more I moved inside of her, the wetter she got. The pussy was so good I couldn't pull out if I wanted to.

"Got damn! You can handle it. You can take this dick, lil mama. Damn, this muthafucka so damn good," I growled, slowing down my pace because I could feel it in the pit of my stomach that I was about to bust. The way she was moving, trying to keep up with me, you could tell that she didn't know what she was doing. But it's the way she's just lying there doing nothing, and the pussy still put a damn chokehold on my damn dick. I've never been inside virgin pussy, but this pussy was the best I've had in my damn life. All you could hear was the sounds of me pounding the fuck outta her, and the moans coming from her beautiful ass lips. I could feel that this might have been the biggest mistake of my fuckin' life. Because it wasn't no way I could go back to normal knowing she possessed this top tier ass pussy.

"Cam! Ohh my God! Something's happening!" she screamed as tears streamed down her face and her body started to shake.

"You cummin, lil mama. Let that shit go!" I commanded in her ear as I pushed so deep that I hit something. I continued to fuck the shit out of Remi until I released the biggest nut of my life. We both laid there for a few minutes in our own thoughts. The more I laid here, the more I wanted to slide back in this girl. I felt like the pussy was calling me, and I damn sure was about to answer it.

Chapter Two

REMI

One month later
I've been working on this chemistry project with my partner Johnathan for the past couple of weeks, and I'm so excited about presenting it at the competition on Monday. If we win, Johnathan and I will get the rest of our tuition paid. I did get some scholarships that cover two years of school, but the last two years are on me. I don't have any help; my mother doesn't really care about me being here in school.

She would rather I be home taking care of her and her drug addiction. My mama is a functioning powder head, and God knows what else she's on. I tried so many times to get her help, but she just won't go into any programs. My dad does the best he can to help me, but he has his wife and kids to take care of as well. One thing I can say about him is he's always calling and checking on me to make sure I'm alright. I started tutoring to make extra money and thank God for that because that's how I take care of myself.

"Do you think we have everything we need, or do you think we need to add something else to it?" Johnathan questioned as we sat under a tree on campus eating some lunch.

"Trust me, there is nothing else we need. I just know we did everything right with this project and I'm so excited." I smiled, wrapping my arms around him in pure joy.

"So, is this nigga the reason you couldn't come help me study for my exam?!" Cam walked up to us, and I was shocked that he approached us like that.

"Cam, what are you talking about?" I asked.

"Oh, so now yo' geeky ass gone sit here and act like you the fuck slow. Ain't shit slow about yo' ass, but your damn walk. You knew I had an exam yesterday, and we were supposed to study over the weekend. You knew how bad I needed to pass that damn exam, so don't sit there looking at this cross-eyed ass nigga like you don't know what the fuck I'm talking about!" He snapped off on me. Tears burned the rim of my eyes, but I refused to let them fall. Cam and I have been in a weird place ever since we had sex.

I knew he wasn't trying to be in a relationship with me, and I promised him that it was nothing to it but sex. I'm not going to lie; I think of being with him every night. I don't know what love feels like because I've never been in love. But if it's like what I see in those romance movies, when the heroine says her heart skipped a beat, then that's me. Every time I see Camron Kassom, my heart skips many beats.

It's been weeks since I saw him because I've been working on my very important project. I also told him all about this project, and just like that, everything we talked about came rushing back to me. Throwing my hands up to my face, I did promise to help him.

12

"Cam, I forgot all about it. I'm so sorry. I swear it wasn't intentional. I'm sure the professor will offer a retake if I speak with him." I tried to plead with him, but the angry look on his face let me know that he wasn't trying to hear that.

"Nah, I'm good. I don't need your help on shit!" he spat, and I swear the venom in his voice shot through my chest and caused pain in my heart. I was fighting back the tears, but I knew I couldn't stop them from falling.

"Don't talk to her like that. Have some damn respect." Johnathan jumped up into Cam's face.

"Nigga, get yo' Karlton lookin' ass outta my face." Cam stepped closer to him.

"Or what, my nigga?! Just because you think I'm this geek just know I'm 'bout that life too! You're not just going to step in her face disrespecting her like that. Take that aggression on out on the person that deserves it." Johnathan looked at him, and even I was taken aback. Johnathan was beyond smart, but he also didn't take any crap from anyone.

"*Take that aggression out on someone that deserves it.* This nigga a bitch!" Cam spat. "You're right! Since you 'bout it, I'm just gone take this aggression out on yo' Captain Save-A- Hoe bitch ass!" Cam swung, hitting him in the jaw and that was it. They were going blow for blow, but eventually, Cam was too much for Johnathan. A crowd started forming around us, and I tried my best to pull them apart, but they were too strong for me. Some of the guys from the football team pulled Cam off Johnathan and rushed him away.

I tried to get Johnathan to let it go, but when campus police showed up, he told them that Cam was the one that hit him. They asked me if I saw what happened, and I just walked away.

There was no way that I could tell on Cam. I knew what this could possibly do to him. If he got kicked out of school, he could mess up his chances of going into the league. I just hate that he came at me like that, and now Johnathan is mad with me. Fuck my life!

Chapter Three

CAM

A month had passed, and nothing between Remi and I was the same. I haven't spoken to her since I beat her nigga the fuck up. That bitch nigga reported me, but later said he thought he got shit confused. I could have gotten suspended from school, and my dad was about to have a damn conniption over the shit. I knew this would give him something to go the fuck off on me about. I love my pop, but he was always down my back, no matter what I did. The school could call and say I was a nickel short on my parking fee and his ass was ready to go to war with me.

"Cam!" I heard someone call my name when I jumped out of my car heading into the pizza shop. When I turned to see who it was, I kept the fuck moving. Looking around the restaurant for my girl, I didn't see her, so I was stuck facing the one person that I was still pissed the fuck off with- Remi. I really didn't have shit to say to her, and that's crazy because I never thought I would feel or say some shit like that about her.

"Cam, please. I need to talk to you for a minute." I let out a frustrated sigh, finally turning to face her.

"Sup?" I looked at her with a blank stare. Shit wasn't supposed to be this way with me and Remi. The exam was really important for me, and I know it's not her fault, but damn, I was depending on her to help me. Ever since she had been hanging with that geeky ass nigga it's been on some Fuck Cam bullshit. The fuck! So, yeah, I'm good on everything about her ass.

"I really need to talk to you; can we sit down and talk?" She questioned.

"Nahh, I'm meeting my girl in a few minutes." I looked at her. I knew that she didn't know that Saniya and I hooked up after shit went north with us.

"Your girl?! Oh ok, but this is important, and I think it's something we should talk about. First, I need to apologize to you. Cam, it wasn't intentional. It really slipped my mind. You know I wouldn't do anything to purposely hurt you. I've always been there to help you with anything you need pertaining to your studies. I didn't expect this to mess up our friendship the way it did." She pushed her glasses up on the bridge of her nose with a concerned look on her face. I wanted to wrap my arms around her 'cause I truly missed lil mama. And if I'm really being honest with myself, my anger didn't have shit to do with her helping me study.

"It's all good." I shrugged.

"Cam, I'm pregnant," she blurted out, and I laughed because what was she trying to say?

"What! You haven't known dude a good two months and you're already letting him hit raw? That shit ain't a good look, lil baby. What about school? You gotta think about shit like that.

16

Thank God we didn't fuck up, 'cause the last damn thing I need is a kid coming and fuckin' up what I got going on right now. I mean, one day I want kids, but a baby isn't a part of the plans right now." I felt bad for her, but that's some shit she gone have to work through on her own. The light in her eyes dimmed, and sadness covered her face.

"Cam, ummm….." She was cut off when Saniya walked up.

"Hey, babe! What's up, Remi?" Saniya walked in between us, wrapping her arms around my neck and pulling me in for a kiss. Damn, what a kiss it was. Shit, by the time I pulled away from my girl, Remi had already walked away. I hope baby girl would be alright with this, but that's some shit she gone have to figure out with her dude.

"What did she want? I thought we had an understanding that you wouldn't talk to her anymore." Saniya pouted, poking her lips out.

"Nah, you had that understanding. Let's get something straight before we go any further. You don't get to tell me who I can and can't be friends with, as long as it's not disrespecting you in any way." The waitress walked up to show us to our table, and she did that shit just in time because I wasn't about to do this shit with Saniya. She hated Remi on some next-level shit, and I couldn't understand why. It was almost as if she was obsessed with the idea of hating her so much.

Not wanting her near me is one thing, but this shit was something different. I'm glad she doesn't know that Remi and I slept together because her ass would really be on some other shit. We did our best to enjoy the rest of our night, but Niya had an attitude most of the night. After dinner, we both went to our own shit, because I wasn't feeling the way she was acting.

I've been laying here for the past four hours thinking about the conversation with Remi. I couldn't get the look in her eyes out of my mind. Looking over at the clock, it was going on seven in the morning. Remi was an early riser anyway. Jumping out of bed, I took care of my hygiene and threw on some clothes. I didn't live on campus, but I only lived about five minutes away. Pulling into the parking lot near her dorm, I headed up to her room. I knocked on the door, and it took a minute, but her room-mate Chrissy answered the door.

"You're a little too late; she's gone," she spoke with an attitude.

"What time will she back?" I asked, trying to look inside, but she was blocking the door.

"She withdrew from school and went back home. No, I don't know why it must be a money thing because you know she didn't win that contest. Somebody reported her and Johnathan saying they cheated or some shit like that. But they didn't cheat on any of that shit. These people at this school weird as fuck. And I almost wanna say you a goofy for treating her like shit when she out here ridin' for yo' rank ass. See, let me calm the fuck down and stop talking, cause I'm ten seconds off yo' ass, the Philly way," she spat, slamming the door in my damn face.

Like what the fuck! *Why would she withdraw from school like that?* I mean, I understand that she was pregnant, but damn, she could have figured that shit out. Remi and I talked about a lot of shit, but her background and family weren't one of them. I knew she was from a small town in South Carolina, but I had no clue where to start. I guess this is the part where I decide if I should even bother. She made the decision to leave and mess up her chances at a good education. As soon as I made it back to my place, my phone started ringing, and it was my mom calling.

18

"Hey, ma."

"Hey, baby. You were heavy on my mind this morning. Are you alright?" She questioned. I sat on the bed, letting out a heavy sigh. I was trying to decide if I want to talk to my mom about Remi or not.

"Yeah, I'm good, ma. I miss you. Are you doing alright?"

"Yes, I'm ok. I'm getting ready to go have breakfast with Grams and Aunt Ari." Before I could respond, my Facetime was going off, I hit the button to answer it because my mom wasn't going to stop until she made sure I was alright. She always knew when shit was off with her kids. She didn't play about her kids or her husband. I smiled when her face appeared on the screen.

"That's always what I love to see, a smile on my baby boy's face. You look tired. Are you getting enough rest?"

"Yeah, I'm good. I just couldn't sleep last night. Mom, it's been months, and you still haven't given me an answer about entering the draft. You know the deadline is coming up, and even though I love it here, I'm ready for this, mom," I pleaded with her.

"I only want the best for you, Cameron. You better promise me that no matter what, you will get that degree. I don't care what degree you choose to get, but I want one, and I want to see you walk across that stage. I give you my permission to enter the draft." She smiled.

"Hell yeah!" I jumped up, full of excitement.

"Cameron, you can talk to your coach about it, but don't make any public announcements until we arrive with your agent. We'll see you in a few days and remember who you're cursing in front of before you do that shit again," my dad stated, as he appeared on the Facetime.

"Yes, sir." Is all I had to say because this was the first time that he's said anything to me in damn near two months. I spoke with my parents for a few minutes longer and then ended the call. I was so damn excited about the news I kind of pushed Remi to the back of my mind. And at that point I was ready to start my new life. I pray that everything works out for Remi and maybe one day I will see her again.

Chapter Four

CAM

Six years later

We just landed in New York and were now on our way to my parents' house.

"You good, bro?" my best friend, Raheim, asked.

"Yeah, I'm good. I appreciate you taking the trip to make sure things go as planned. When do you go back to Atlanta?" I asked.

"I'll be here with you guys until after the interview. I want to make sure things go right. Remember, you only have to answer questions that you feel comfortable with. The same goes for you, Saniya," Rah explained, and my fiancée turned her nose up at him. Saniya and I have been together since college, and I asked her to marry me about a year ago. She's pissed because Rah suggested that when we get married, she signs a prenup.

She hates that prenup talk, but oh, we 'bout to definitely get deep in the conversation. So, she about to be one mad ass. Prenups were something that the Kassom family didn't believe in. The men in our family loved and trusted their women and vice versa. I'm not the trusting traditional Kassom you're used to hearing about. I rock a little differently. I guess that's why my pop and I bump heads so much. Don't get it fucked up, I love the guy, and I'll go to war about him every time.

But it's times that we're at war with each other. He's so damn strict on me and believes that I'm supposed to do what he says when he says it. I'm grown as fuck, and I operate on my own time and rules. That shit kills me because he's never acted this way with Ju, Kari, and Laila. So, what is it about me that always has his ass on go? I will never understand it, which keeps me from coming home all the time. Mom always says out of all of her kids; I reminded her the most of my dad. My mannerisms, the way I walk, talk, and of course, my looks. It was true, I was the spitting image of my pops. You would think he had a clone. The only difference is I'm a little taller and more muscular than he was.

"Does your family know that the camera crew is coming with us tonight and that the cameras will be on and rolling when we get inside?" Rah questioned as we pulled into the driveway my parents' home.

"Nah, I figured I'll tell them when we get inside." I smiled. I knew this shit would piss my dad off because he likes to prepare for everything, but they just asked me about the camera crew last night. I agreed to it, and the extra five mil they added to the contract for doing this exclusive interview helped persuade me.

"Nigga, you're playing with fire. You know damn well your family needs to be prepared and talked to for a while before putting a camera in their damn face. Especially your grandmother."

"Tuh, you could never prepare that ghetto mess," Saniya stated. I whipped my head in her direction so fast I almost broke my shit.

"Niya, say something else about my grandmother, or my family in general, and you will be going back on the next commercial flight to Atlanta. Don't fuck with me about my family. I don't disrespect you or your family, so don't do it with mine," I spat.

The security check on all the cars was complete, and the gates opened. Rah looked over at me, shaking his head because he believed that Saniya is with me for the money and fame. Raheim has been my boy since high school. When I made my pick to LSU, he applied and got in as well. He graduated with his law degree and now represents me, and tons of other athletes in the NFL and NBA. Since I got drafted, I've been playing for the Falcons and was the number one pick. I'm the highest-paid quarterback in the league and the most sought-after player.

We're playing in the playoffs, and next weekend is the last game, which will determine which teams will be playing in the Super Bowl. Black Excellence Television is one of the largest television networks in the country. I wanted all of my family to be a part of the interview tomorrow. That included our extended family as well. When we pulled up to the house, the cars packed the driveway.

I assumed all the family was here waiting for me to get home. Something is telling me that maybe I shouldn't have agreed to the cameras following me. Or maybe I should've told my family that the cameras were going to be on. This might be a fuckin' disaster; I could feel it. The moment I got out of the car, Mark, the chief camera guy, placed a mic on me and told me to just act natural. I think his ass should run inside and tell my family that shit. Now that we're here, I'm having second thoughts about these damn cameras being on. I can only pray that my family behaves. When we walked into the house, I could hear them laughing and talking. I walked into the room, and my mom jumped up from her seat.

"Cam! I'm so glad to see you. I've missed you so much, baby!" my mom wrapped her arms around me.

"Welcome home, son." My dad walked up to hug me.

"Hey, dad. It's good to be home." I smiled.

"Sup, Neph? You ready to ball the fuck out next weekend?" my uncle Zelan questioned, walking up to hug me, followed by the rest of my family.

"You already know what it is, Unc." I smiled.

"Hey, everybody," I greeted them all.

"What's up, bro?" Ju, and Kari both came to hug me.

"Sup, y'all? Where is Laila?" I asked, looking around the room.

"She'll be here in time for the interview tomorrow. Hey, Saniya. How are you?" My mom asked, smiling over at Niya.

"I'm good." She smiled, and I knew it was gone be some shit.

"Oh, she playing with the wrong mother, 'cause fuckin' with mine will cause you to get a bull…." Rah cut Kari off because we all knew she was about to go in on Niya.

"Ummmm, nephew, why the crew here to setup already? They sholl wanna be prepared to talk to yo' ass. Y'all don't know how to come on regular people time 'cause we not gone talk to y'all asses tonight! What the hell are those cameras for?" Uncle Gabe asked, walking up to dap me up.

"There's some hoes in this house! There's some hoes in this house! Certi-

24

fied freak seven days a week. Ayyyyeeeeee! Chile, I still got them Megan and Cardi knees, babbbbyyyy! Y'all can call me Lai the Juice Slayer! Yessss, my grandson is home. Now we can get this party started!" My grandma Lai walked into the room rapping *Wap by Cardi B and Meg Thee Stallion* with a blunt hanging from her mouth and a glass of liquor in her hand. The camera crew turned to her ass so quick one of the guys almost hit the floor.

"Why they turn them cameras on her like that?" Uncle Gabe questioned.

"Cam, are those cameras live?" My dad asked, walking up with his face turned into a frown.

"Yes, they're live. They wanted to follow me around for a day before the interview.

"Awww hell nawl! Mmmm, mmmm, Lai don't do cameras." Grams turned her head, trying to cover her damn face. Ummmm, it's too late for all that shit. They done seen it all from her ass.

"So, let me get this shit straight. This nigga done brought in cameras to the largest drug organization and serial killing ass family on this side of the globe. Tru, Ion think this the type of interview we need to be doing; these niggas bout to go to jail. We need to end our friendship with they ass! Nowadays, these judges are giving you life for parking fuckin' tickets. Imagine what they gone give us for running a crime organization. Mmmm, mmmmm!

That's why I pay all me and Gia's tickets when they come. I just let Layah's shit pile up 'cause it might be cheaper if I let the state pick her ass up. That means she ain't gone need no clothes, car, no insurance, or groceries from my ass. How you got a job and you still beggin! They gone give her lil' homely ass all she needs behind bars; a hot and a muthafuckin' cot." I heard Uncle

25

Gabe talking to Uncle Truth. I swear I wanted to laugh, but now wasn't the time. Thank God the crew wasn't paying him any attention.

"I need those cameras off right damn now!" My dad demanded, walking up to the crew. He was pissed, and I knew we were going to have words over this. I should have talked to him and mom about it. I meant to talk to them when we got inside, but I was so happy to see everyone, and I forgot about it. Pulling Mark to the side, I told him to cut everything he had involving my family and just let everyone know when the cameras were recording. Every time the cameras went by Grandma Lai, she ducked, as if she was wiping some shit down. If we didn't get it together quick, this interview was about to be the craziest shit on television.

Chapter Five

REMI

I had to come home to South Carolina because my mom's sister, Katrina, passed away, and her funeral services was earlier today. A knock on my door quickly jolted me from my thoughts.

"Hey, baby. The food is ready, do you want me to fix you a plate and bring it to you?" My mom asked, smiling.

"No, I'm fine right now, mom. If you don't mind, can you fix Kaleb and Kamryn a plate?"

"Yeah, I'll fix it. Pootah, I really enjoyed having you and my grandkids here with me this week. I'm gonna miss y'all when you leave tomorrow."

"We enjoyed you too, Ma. Maybe you can come visit us before the summer is over. I think the kids would love a visit from their grandma." I smiled at her.

"I would love that." She smiled and closed the door. My mom has done a complete 180 ever since her grandkids were born. I remember going through so much while pregnant, and she

27

promised that we would get through it together. She even promised that she would be clean by the time I had my baby. That was before we knew I was having twins. It was a tough time, but she did it, and I'm so proud of her. The kids love everything about their grandmother.

"Mommy, Kaleb keeps calling me a dummy because I can't name all the presidents. I don't care who all them is 'cause they don't know who I am. I can't remember all that; it hurts my brain." Kamryn pouted, holding her head. My kids are both the smartest little things ever. They're five years old, and I can't imagine my life without them. Kaleb is me all day, and Kamryn has so much attitude, but she's smart as well. I think she got that attitude from her dad. Kaleb has a special gift, and I could see it when he was about three years old. He was able to speak properly. There was no baby gibberish. He was having full-blown kid talks with me. Kamryn took a little longer, but by the time she was four, she was the same way. Kaleb is being tested for the gifted in a couple of months, and even though I'm excited for him, I'm not sure that I want to remove him from kids his age. Kaleb walked into the room, and my kids reminded me of their dad's mom so much it was a little scary.

"Look, it's my daddy!" Kamryn shouted, pointing at the television. They were talking about Cam on Sports Center. I saw on his Instagram earlier that he was in New York visiting his family, and I saw that he was with that bitch Saniya. She never liked me, and after seeing that Cam was with her that night back in college, I hated her existence. They knew exactly who their dad was, and it broke my heart knowing that they would never meet him. Kamryn asked for her dad often, and Kaleb would mention him ever so often. I know it's fucked up, but I tried to talk to Cameron about my pregnancy. When he said he was happy he didn't mess up with me, and that kids weren't in his plans, that got to me.

I didn't want to mess anything up for him, and I damn sure didn't want me being pregnant to stop his plans. Leaving school and figuring out for what would be next, was something I had to deal with. My road wasn't the easiest, but I did what I had to do to make a great life for me and my kids. My dreams of being a doctor didn't work, so once I had my babies and got myself together, I went back to school locally and got my master's in journalism. I loved it. There were so many times I thought about reaching out to Camron, but what he said that night in the pizza shop resonated with me. The kids ran out of the room, almost knocking my cousin Shanae down.

Shanae walked into the room with a plate. "Girl, you need to eat. I just told Aunt Joyce I didn't see you eat anything all day. Now eat some of this food, 'cause I damn sure don't got time for your ass falling the hell out and they think we did something to your ass. Hell nawl, I got too many warrants! Leave them people's ambulance and police cars where the fuck they at 'cause I'm bound to ride in one of 'em. Ain't nobody got time for that shit." She shook her head, sitting down on the bed.

"Shan! Why the hell you out here running from the police?" I fell out laughing because this shit was funny.

"Girl, these niggas on my roster be out here fuckin' with me. I got into a fight with one of 'em last summer, and the nigga called the police, and I went to jail. I ended up having to do community service and shit. They had my ass out there cleaning trash in the parks. The fuck I look like cleaning some damn trash? Girl, I was pissed. When I saw his ass again, me and mama jumped his piss po' fish mouth havin' ass. Mama in the dirt now, so they can't catch her. But my ass is good as got if I'm not careful. The nigga gone call me and say if I give him some pussy, he gone tell them folk he made a mistake.

If I ever give that nigga this pussy again, that shit gone be laced with some shit to lay his ass down forever, bihhhh! His ass was just slow, and I can't fuck with slow niggas. If I tell yo' ass that you my nigga on Friday, and everything is all you on Friday, why you out here trying to fuck me and my Thursday nigga shit up, on Thursday! That shit don't make no fuckin' sense. Like nigga, if you need help remembering yo' day of the week, I can set that shit up on yo calendar or some shit. 'Cause I need him to stay the fuck on track. Like this one time, the inconsistent nigga tried to come over on a Sunday, and ion get down like that at the fuck all. Like don't come fuckin' with me on the lawd's day. That's the day for me and my Sunday, nigga. It would only be fitting to fuck a passa on the lawd's day.

Shit, I'm trying to get closer to gawd and that fine nigga in the pool pit. I'm about to be the first lady over at Good Sheppard Church of Christ Mt. Zion Holy Tabernacle Ebenezer Baptist Church! Chilleeee, them Sunday go to meeting heifers don't like my ass 'cause they know I'm giving they passa all this ill nah nah. Shit, when they're taking up the pastoral offering that shit comes right to me. I got that nigga wrapped around my pinky toe and my pussy lips. Praise gawd!" She fell out laughing, and my ass was rolling on the bed, trying to catch my breath. I swear my cousin was a fool, and she didn't care about shit. Kamryn came back into the room, and just as she walked in, they were saying that Camron was the best and highest paid athlete to ever grace the NFL. They say if he wins the playoffs, and wins the Super Bowl, he's going to be a golden ticket and unstoppable.

"Mommy, look. It's my daddy again!" Kam called out.

"Girl, why that damn baby thinks pretty boy Cam is her daddy?" Shan questioned, looking at me with the side-eye.

I shrugged, looking away from her ass. "I don't know. She just started saying it one day, and ever since then, she's been calling him that." I nervously chuckled.

"Cause babbby, I wish his fine rich ass was my daddy and not the one that nurtures. I wanna be able to call him Zaddy when his ass is hittin' that shit from the back. Baby boy can get it, and I mean that on my dead mama we just dropped in the dirt. His ass can be my sexy Monday Madness since I don't got nobody on that day." This girl had me in tears because I've never heard no shit like this before. I ate, drank, and cut the fool with my cousin for the rest of the day.

I'm nothing like I was in college. I don't act the same, nor do I dress the same. I got life and my best friend Zori to thank for that. It was a little after nine by the time I got the kids to sleep and now I'm in bed myself. We had a 5 a.m flight back to New York. It was always a dream of mine to live in the Big Apple. So when Zori called me about interning as a journalist at her job, I jumped on it, and me and my babes were headed to New York. I truly can't thank my friends enough for all they do for me and the kids. If it wasn't for Zori and Johnathan, I don't know if I would have made it.

They both eventually found me after I left school, and we've been rocking together ever since. I apologized to Johnathan for not having his back that day with Cam, and he forgave me. Zori and Johnathan are Kaleb and Kamryn's godparents, and my babies were crazy about them. Cam was heavy on my mind for some reason, and I really hoped everything was alright with him. My phone was ringing, and I grabbed it off the nightstand.

"Zori boo, what's going on with you?" I greeted when I answered the call.

"Hey, bae. I need a big favor from you. Jason just called me ten minutes ago, saying that he needs me to do an interview because the journalist that was set to do it is sick. Jason gave me free rein to bring whomever I wanted to help me on set, and I told him I wanted you. I don't know who it is because this shit is supposedly top secret until it airs. What time does your flight land?" She questioned.

"Wow! Thank you, Zori. But I'm not sure if I can do it because I don't have anyone to watch the kids tomorrow. Unless Johnathan can do it, I will call him in the morning and let you know. What time do I need to be there?" I asked her as I adjusted in bed.

"No later than one. I need to brief you, and then we have to get the person we're interviewing prepped and ready. Heads up, Jason will be on site with us, so you definitely have to be on point." Zori and I finished talking over the details, and after our call, I drifted off to sleep. Before I knew it, the alarm clock was going off. I got up, waking the kids up to get them dressed. My mom knocked on the door a few minutes later.

"I set my clock because I knew you would need help getting them together." I smiled because she was right, I did need a little help, and I was grateful. Kammy is such a diva in the mornings, and her attitude has me ready to pull my hair out. Once we got everything together and the kids in the car, I said my goodbyes to my mom and cousin. They both promised to make the trip to New York next month. It was going on nine in the morning when we got back in the city and on our way home.

"Mommy, can we have a snack, please?" Kammy begged as soon as we got settled at home. I lived near Central Park in a nice three-bedroom condo. It was close to work and the kid's daycare. I was excited about that because it took us no time to get to and from there each day. Kammy thinks her and her brother are supposed to get snacks daily. When it comes to ice cream and cookies, she thinks we own Haagan-Daz and Mrs. Fields.

"One snack each, and if you're good for your god dad, I will take you and your brother to get Ice cream tomorrow." I kissed her cheek.

"Ok, mommy. I'm going to be the best daughter ever. Now I don't know about your son; he's a little weird sometimes. If he acts up, that has nothing to do with me." She put her hand on her nonexisting hip. I decided to try to take an hour nap before it was time to head out to the location of the interview. Zori sent the address over early this morning, and I'm so glad that Jonathan was able to watch the kids.

It was a little after eleven, and I had just finished getting dressed. That nap I was supposed to take never happened. I heard the doorbell, and I knew it was Johnathan. I walked into the living room to open the door for him.

"Damn! You sure you don't want to take this past our friend-ship level? I already told you I'll kick Nell to the side any day for you." He kissed my cheek.

"Hush, you know that's not happening. I love our friendship too much to mess it up." I smiled, nudging him.

"Daddy Johnathan!" both of the kids ran to him, and he lifted them both into his arms. They loved Johnathan, and he loved them so much. They know he's not their real father, but they both just started calling him that. At first, I tried to stop them from doing it, but the kids just wouldn't stop.

"Hey, princess!" Jonathan tickled her, and she bent over in laughter.

"What's up, champ?" he tickled Kaleb, and he fell into a fit of laughter.

"Have they eaten? It's a nice day out, and I'm going to take them to have some lunch and maybe go to the park," he said to me, and I'm sure they will go shopping as well.

"No, they haven't eaten, and I should be done around seven, eight at the latest," I told him. I went to gather my things so that I could leave. I leaned down to love on my babies, and about five minutes later, I was out the door. I haven't had a man since sleeping with Cameron. I know it sounds crazy, and the only person that knows that is Zori. She's always trying to hook me up just so I could get my shit off, but I think that whole ordeal with Cam and me getting pregnant just messed me up. I know he didn't promise me anything, and it was me that was persistent, but that shit just took something out of me.

Then it's the fact that I thought we were friends, and he treated me like crap in the end. It took me almost an hour to get to the address. I couldn't believe that this place was this beautiful. The mansion seemed to be as long as a couple of football fields. This place was freaking beautiful. I couldn't wait to get on the other side of the gate to see it. All I could think of was who the hell lived here. It had to be a celebrity that was bigger than life. It took me about twenty minutes to get cleared at the security gate, and they finally let me through. Were we interviewing with the president because that's how deep these security people were? I saw our crew going inside the house, so I got out and rang the doorbell. I texted Zori to let her know that I was at the door.

"How can I help you?" The maid asked with a smile.

"Hello, I'm Remi Blake. I'm here with the Black Excellence team." I smiled.

"Oh yes, ma'am. They're in the family room four doors down

the hall on the right," she stated and allowed me to enter the beautiful home. I've never in my life been in anything like this, and I couldn't imagine having this much money to afford anything like this. This family is truly blessed. I was walking down the hall and I saw someone I thought I knew. As he got closer, I remembered him from a day camp that Kaleb went to, and he was the host. He stopped and looked at me with the same 'I know you from somewhere' look.

"Hi, do I know you?" He asked.

"I'm sorry, I was thinking the same thing. Were you at The Kids Like Me Foundation camp last summer? My son Kaleb was one of the kids there, and he had a spelling battle with the host." I asked him.

"Yes, I was. Yesssss, Kaleb! That was my little smart buddy. I often speak about Kaleb and how smart he is. How is he?" He asked, and just as I was about to answer, Zori came rushing out of the room.

"I need to talk to you right now. I'm sorry, Mr. Kassom. Please excuse us." She grabbed my arm and pulled me back down the hall.

"Wait... did you just say Kassom?" I asked as my heart rate sped up. I never knew his last name, and I'm still trying to remember his damn first. "Is he related to Cam, Zori?" I stopped and looked at her.

"Yes, he's Cam's brother, and this is Cam's parents' house. Remi, I had no idea that he was who we were interviewing. I just saw him five minutes ago for the first time. Look, I can handle this interview. I know how you feel and what this could cause in your life. You can leave now before he sees...."

"Remi!" We heard a voice call my name and my body started to tremble a little. I felt like someone was squeezing my heart back and forth I was so nervous to face him. His voice was deeper than what it was when we were in college, but it was a voice I would never forget. Turning to face him slowly as I tried to gather myself.

"Cameron! Wow! It's been such a long time. How have you been?" I nervously asked him, but he didn't answer he just stared at me and seemed to be in deep thought. I never expected to see him ever again. This man was beautiful. He looked so much better in person than he did on television. My God, the man above took his time making and developing him.

Chapter Six

CAM

Fuck! Is it really her?! This girl looks nothing like Remi. The glasses were gone, her hair was bone straight, hanging down to the middle of her back, and I'm not going to even talk about the hips, ass, and titties on this woman. She was a fuckin' bombshell and was beautiful as fuck! What the fuck!

"Remi! Are you alright?" Zori asked her, jolting her out of her thoughts. I couldn't say shit because I was still trying to pull my heart outta my ass.

She cleared her throat. "Yeah, I'm good," she replied, but her gaze was still on me. I'm not sure where Remi has been all of these years, but I've definitely thought about her and wondered if she was doing okay. There were many times that I wanted to look her up just to make sure she was cool. It's been over six years and can't believe how she's changed. Damn!

"How have you been, Remi? It's been a long time. I came to look for you the next day and Zori told me you had left school. I hate that shit happened to you, and you had to do all of that. I know you're a doctor by now."

"No, things didn't go as planned for me, so I took another direction. I'm one of the lead journalists in the country," she revealed, and I was a little taken back because being a doctor is all she talked about.

"Oh yeah, that's dope as fuck. I'm glad shit worked out for you. How is your kid?" I asked her, and before she could answer, Saniya walked up.

"Who are they, bae?" Niya asked, wrapping her arms around me.

"Saniya, don't stand yo' ass there as if you don't know who the fuck we are. This bitch 'bout to make me lose my job. I couldn't stand her ass then and damn sure can't stand this hoe now." Zori was pissed, and the producer dude pulled her off with him. That could've been the end of this interview, but I knew the history of Zori, Saniya, and Remi. And the fact that Zori is right; Saniya knows who they are. Shit, but as fine as Remi done got maybe she really don't know that it's Remi.

"Niya, this is Remi from college. I know you remember my tutor and friend Remi," I told her.

"Ohhh yeah, Remi the nerdy chick. Hey, girl! I see life been treating you alright. Damn, I guess you finally got you a lil' body or whatever 'cause in college, girl, yo' ass was a mess. I guess what they say about time changes all things. Time definitely helped you a little." She laughed, and if I was into knocking the shit out of women, I swear my girl would be the first one I sucker slide in the damn throat.

"Time has definitely allowed me to grow and glo gracefully. But you, not so much, baby. It looks as if you could use a gym to tighten up a little, and the botox must not be working on your face. I see a little wrinkles. It was nice seeing you again, Cam. Congratulations on your success." She smiled and walked her beautiful ass away, and I couldn't turn away even if I wanted to.

"What the fuck! Are you going to stand there and watch her ass or are you going to be respectful and go check that dusty ass bitch for talking to your fiancée like that?!" Saniya angrily spat.

"Slutville! Who the fuck is you talkin' to like that! Grandson! Who she talking to 'cause babbby, I know it ain't you? You might think I'm old and can't do shit, but I will tear that ass up, lil girl! I don't play about that one!" My grandma fussed all up in Saniya's face.

"You're being drastic!" Saniya waved her off.

"I'mma show yo' ass drastic. Drastic gone get yo' ass drastically dropped in a casket! You betta ask about me! I'm the muthafuckin' queen of '*snitches get put in ditches*. We bag 'em and tag em' round this bitch! It's gone be Gang Bang crew errrday all muthafuckin' day. And that's on Mary had a lil lamb and the bitch's snowy white ass feet! My guns gone be blazin' 'til my casket drop!" Grams told her. I tried my best not to laugh, but that shit was hard.

"Grams, that's a lil' harsh. Don't talk to her like that." The slap upside my head let me know that she wasn't trying to hear shit I had to say.

"Nigga, shut yo' slow ass up. A blind man can see this hoe for the streets and your damn bank account!" My grandmother didn't like Saniya. She said she was a money hungry hoe, and so is her mama. Those were my Grams' words. I tried to take up for my girl, but Grams always threatened me. The part that had me in a fit of laughter is when she popped Saniya upside the head too but didn't notice the camera crew standing there.

When she did notice them, she pulled a hoodie over her

head, and slid some dark ass glasses on, trying to hide her face. This shit was hilarious. Hell, I didn't even notice that she had on a hoodie, but now that I think of it, she's been rocking' one since last night. I looked over at the camera guy.

"We'll go over the recording with you, sir, for any deletions," Mark said to me.

"I think that's best for you, son. You ever seen a private zoo before? We got one in the back. Maybe I can show it to you later tonight," Grams told Mark.

"Yes ma'am. The Zoo sounds like a lot of fun. I would love for you to show me." He smiled as they walked off together. Mark didn't have the camera on her, so she was cool. Saniya stormed off, heading to the family room.

"That nigga 'bout to die and he don't even know it. Just cause old ladies seem nice, you gotta watch out for the ones that's old, but still look a lil' young. Cause Ma gone have that nigga hanging from the gator rack, right after she slit his throat!" Uncle Gabe said to Uncle Truth, shaking his head. I knew some of the things that my family is into; I'm not that blind. My parents tried to keep me from that part of their life, but I know what it is.

When I walked into the family room Zori, Remi, and their team were going over the interview process with my family. I couldn't stop looking at this girl. That was some dangerous shit because I'm about to get married to Saniya, and I love my girl.

"Cam, we will be ready to go at four. Zori is the lead journalist, and she will be doing the interview with you," Jason pulled me aside to let me know what was happening.

"I thought Remi was a lead journalist. Why isn't she doing it?" I asked him, and this nigga burst into laughter.

"Where did you get that from? She's not ready for interviews yet." He chuckled again, looking over at Remi.

"Get her ready, because either she does my interview, or we don't do it at all." I looked over at him.

"I suggest you get her ready because he's serious," Raheim told him.

"What?! We're paying you twenty million to do this interview. You would blow that over her?" He asked me in disbelief.

"In a heartbeat! Get her ready for the interview!" I walked off and headed out of the room without saying anything to anyone. That lil' quirky ass nigga pissed me the fuck off. Damn nigga, you need to shake back 'cause this girl got you about ready to risk it all, and she's only been in the fuckin' house for thirty minutes. I had to go get my mind right before the interview because right now, shit was all off with me.

Chapter Seven

REMI

There were so many things running through my mind. I can't believe that Cam was still with Saniya. Nothing about that evil bitch has changed. All I know is she needs to keep that shit cute with me. I'm a very intelligent woman, but I'm not that same timid person I was back in college. These hands definitely changed and will drag that hoe quick. I've maintained my peace, and I damn sure don't want her ratchet ass disturbing that for me.

"Zori, Remi, can I speak to you both?" Jason pointed and walked out into the hall.

"What's going on?" Zori asked him.

"Listen, there's been a change in plans. Mr. Kassom wants the interview to be held by Remi." He looked in my direction and my damn heart hit the floor.

"What! I can't do that. This interview belongs to Zori, and I will never do that to her," I expressed.

"Oh, you can, and you will," Zori stated.

"I'm not prepared to interview him or his family." I was nervous as hell. Why would he ask for me to do this?!

"I will help you with your interview questions. Wardrobe is here and I'm sure they have something in your size. We need to get you into hair and makeup right now. We start in two hours," Zori said to me. For the next hour, I got my hair and make-up done while Zori helped me get ready. I felt bad because I knew how bad she wanted something like this to happen in her career. Even though we know Cam, he's a really big deal.

"Ok, you're all set." The makeup artist smiled, and I stood from my seat. This entire thing was eating at me, and I felt so damn bad. I pulled Zori to the side just to apologize once more.

"Zori, I'm so sorry about this. I know how badly you wanted a big gig like this, and I swear this was never my intention." Leave it to Cam to cause chaos in a situation.

"I promise you everything is all good. Ok, family, it's time," Zori told them, and everyone took their perspective place. Cam and Saniya walked into the room a few minutes later, and my heart skipped a beat.

"Remi, you got this, babe. You've talked on live television many times, so this should be no different," she whispered. I sighed and took my seat.

"Alright, everyone, we're live in 5,4,3,2,1..."

"Welcome to Black Excellence, and I'm your host, Remi Blake. Today I have the honor and pleasure of speaking with none other than Cameron Kassom and The Kassom family. Well, Cam, thank you for joining me."

"It's a pleasure to be here, Remi. Thank you for having me." He smiled.

"You have been a force in this game since you were drafted,

and now your team is undefeated. Many believe that your team is going all the way, and you will get them there."

"Nah, there's no I in team. I couldn't do any of the things I do without my team. We're one and that's how I've always seen it. Those guys are a part of my family." He smiled, and my damn heart melted. I turned to his mom and dad.

"Mr. and Mrs. Kassom, how was Cam as a child? Did you expect the greatness that he possesses?" I questioned.

"Cam has always been my baby boy. Sometimes I forget that he's all grown up, and my husband or Cam will remind me that I don't have babies anymore. I knew he was destined for greatness when he was just a baby. He's always been determined to make us proud." Ciera smiled, looking over at her son.

"Mr. Kassom, anyone would be proud of the accomplishments their child makes of this stature. I know you're bursting with admiration, and very proud knowing the world is talking, loving, and rooting for your son. It's always the parent that notices their child's talents. When did you notice Cam's talents, and how proud has Cam made you through the years?" I asked him, and it looked as if he was reflecting, so I waited for him to respond.

"I personally noticed Cam's talents when he was in elementary. He loved watching football with me and his uncles here. He expressed that he wanted to play football and asked if they had teams for kids his age. I believe he was in the fourth grade. So, of course, we placed him in Pop Warner. I grew up being a part of the Pop Warner community, and so I wanted my child to experience Pop Warner as well. Those coaches took time with those kids, and that's what I wanted for Cam, and he loved it.

Cam would probably say that my Pop doesn't care, or he's always hard on me. I hate that he thinks that way because I love my son. I've always been hard on him because I wanted him to be a better man than me. Cam is fortunate enough to know that he didn't need any of this to be rich; he was born into wealth. I wanted him to choose his craft because he wanted it for himself. He's had some stumbling blocks along the way, but he's achieved so much.

When my wife had Cameron, there were many promises I made to my infant son. One of those promises was to teach him how to love and be loved, values, hard work, and compassion for others. I taught the same values to my other children, but with Cam, I felt like I needed to be more hands-on and give a little more attention to. His brother and sisters taught me the lessons of watching your kids just a little more." He chuckled.

"You ain't told no damn lies caussssse baebbbayyyy ..... You know what? I'mma just hush," his grandma stated, and the entire family burst into laughter.

"To your other question on how proud I am of my son. I'm very proud of you, son. Just continue to apply those values that your mother and I instilled in you to your life. I love you, my boy." Cam's dad looked over at him as he spoke, and when I saw the tear fall from Cameron's eye, I knew he needed that from his dad.

He stood from his seat and walked over to his dad. That moment caused a few tears. From his mother, aunts, and sisters. I asked some questions with the rest of his family, and I moved on to the private interview with Cam. Unfortunately, his fiancé was with him for the first ten minutes.

"Cam, I see that you're planning a summer wedding with your beautiful longtime girlfriend, Saniya Morris." I smiled, but under my breath, I was calling this hoe all kinds of bitches.

"Yes, and I'm truly excited about that. Niya has been with me since I entered the league, and she makes life easier for me. I love her for that." Hearing him say that caused a pain to shoot through my chest. I couldn't even force myself to smile. I gave a half-smile and moved on.

"Saniya, how proud are you of Cam?" I asked because I damn sure wasn't going to ask her about her wedding plans.

"I'm super proud of my man, girl! He makes me the happiest woman alive, and I can't wait to marry this man this summer in the Maldives." She smiled, leaning in to kiss Cam. I guess he got a glimpse of that millisecond frown because I couldn't hide it. He cleared his throat and ended the kiss. After a few more irrelevant questions, Saniya left and moved to the side with the rest of the family. And now it was just me and Cameron. I adjusted in my seat to get comfortable.

"Cam, what's your earliest football memory?"

"Getting my first 88-yard pass to Shawn Gregg for a touchdown in high school, and now I'm just unstoppable with it," he joked, and we both laughed.

"Was there a time you felt like you wouldn't accomplish your career goals? How did you get back on track?"

"Hell yeah, there were many times I didn't think I would make it. My freshman year of college was chaos and caused a great deal of issues athletically and academically. I got back on track because I had this super smart young lady that helped me through it all. And I owe her so many things, an apology being the first. She was my best friend, and I miss that with her." He looked at me and it was the most uncomfortable moment I've ever experienced. I was literally stuck.

"Whewww chile! You might have a lil' trouble on yo' hands, Cruella cause babbby that sounds like more than best friend love to me. I'm just saying but carry on with the show." I heard his grandmother speak, but it wasn't loud enough to be heard on air.

"Who is your favorite player?"

"I have too many to just name one." He smiled.

"Where do you see yourself post football?"

"Married to the love of my life and having plenty of babies."

"Do you have hobbies or interests outside of sports?" I asked.

"Some of my hobbies and interests, I wouldn't dare say on national television. But one of them is mentoring high school students."

"That's amazing, Cameron." I smiled.

"In your journey to the NFL, do you have any regrets?" I asked him, and it was my last question.

"Not having my best friend with me." There was that uncomfortable feeling again.

"Everything happens for a reason. Maybe your best friend wasn't supposed to be on this ride with you. Maybe your best friend backed away to let you live your life freely without any interruption. Some people are only meant to walk with you for a season. That's just how life goes sometimes. Mr. Cam Kassom, it was a pleasure to have you on the show, and I wish you and your team continued success on your path to the Super Bowl. The best of luck to you!"

"And that's a wrap," The producer called out and everyone clapped it up. I stood from the chair and got some devious smiles from some of the women in Cam's family and the look of death from Saniya.

"Yessss lawd. Is all of these damn cameras off 'cause I need me a damn blunt. Every damn where I go one of them shits is right there. Y'all asses seemed to follow me the most. I felt like I was being discriminated on. The only one I liked following me was that lil chocolate one right there. Yessss gawd! That lil baby fine. The things I would do to you if I wasn't already married," Ms. Laila told him, and everyone fell out laughing.

I couldn't believe she said that, but I could tell she was the life of the party and I loved her. She was a very beautiful woman, and I couldn't believe how old she was. She really didn't look like she was over fifty. "That's nasty as hell. That nigga don't want that cobweb! Ma, stop trying to throw that old shit on these niggas. You don't got what they want," Zelan told her and more laughter erupted.

"They damn sholl don't want that shit. Ma, that shit might turn to dust as soon as a nigga touch it, hell nawl! These young niggas want them a new age chick. You know I heard they got new tricks in the 22. I heard they out here putting y'all to shame, spinnin' on the D with no hands and shit. Now that's that new new shit I'm talkin' 'bout." Mr. Gabe laughed.

"I wonder what mom would say if she saw this video," His daughter said to him.

"And I wonder what the cops would say when I turn yo' draw full of tickets ass in. I hope they come get you. I swear I'm leaving 'yo' don't wanna leave the nest ass' in there," Gabe said to her.

"I don't know where you got that from. I don't have no tick-ets," she fussed.

"Yes, the hell you do, cause I hid them and left them shits unpaid in hopes they would come get yo' ass. You eat too damn much and want too much of my damn money. You can't go shopping like normal people do when it's a sale. Every time Macy's have Friends and Family day, you act like you too damn good to shop there. So, yeah, the people need to come pick you up, and I'm only putting a hundred dollars on yo' commissary."

Gabe shook his head. We all were in a fit of laughter because who says that to their daughter. It was as if that's all they did at home was argue.

"You know God don't like weird and ugly, ugly!" She blurted.

"And he ain't too fond of broke jailbirds. Boom!" He licked his tongue. I swear this family needed to go on a comedy stage. They were hilarious.

"It was a great interview, Cam. Congratulations to you." I held my hand out for him to shake it.

"You did amazingly well yourself." He smiled. As he placed his hand into mine to shake it, a bolt of electricity shot through me, and I snatched away. I guess Zori saw what was going on and pulled me out of the room.

"Girlllll, this dude had no fucks to give about his fiancée being in the room," Zori stated.

"He only said that because we were friends, Zori. I don't think it's anything else. Look, I need to get out of here. Can I take off now and you cover for me?" I asked her.

"Yeah, I got you. Remi, you did an amazing job. This interview is going to set the bar high for you." She hugged me, and I hoped she was right. Once I got into my car and pulled out of the gates, I was able to breathe a sigh of relief.

Chapter Eight

KARI

Two Days Later

I love being home with my family, and the best part of it all is all of my siblings are home at the same time. That hasn't happened in years. It was always one of us missing. Laila came walking into the family room.

"Hey, sissy. Where is everyone?" She asked.

"Mom, dad and the rest of the crew are out back cooking on the grill. Cam, Saniya, and JuJu are getting dressed so that we can go to the mall. Are you coming with us?" I asked.

"Yes, I wish my husband was able to join in on all the festivities. But he's training for his upcoming fight." Laila pouted.

"The same here. Jah isn't due back home until next week."

"Mom! Can we go swimming?" Paisley asked, walking into the room.

"Yes, all of y'all can swim, but you need to talk to Papa first, Pai. You know how he gets when you guys are unsupervised,

50

and you're the oldest. So, you know what that means," I replied.

"Yes ma'am." She turned and left the room in search for her grandfather.

"Cam told me that he and Nigel have something setup for an exclusive interview with Sports Center." She went to the bar and poured a drink. Laila had been drinking more than I've ever seen her drink before.

"Laila, you've been drinking a lot since you've been home. Is everything ok?" I wanted to know because she really was going in since she's been here.

"I'm good. I drink, but I don't overdo it. I promise I'm good. I'm just enjoying the fact that I'm home with the family. We need to go hang out at dad's club before we all go back to our perspective homes. Besides, you know I just had my fourth baby, just let me live a little." She laughed, and I understood where she was coming from. I had three kids, she had four, and JuJu has three. Cam is twenty-six and doesn't have any kids. I'm thankful that he was careful to not have any kids, especially with his so-called girl. I swear if she keeps trying my mom, I'm gone dirt nap her ass. I'm trying to get comfortable in my newly retired life, but my guns are still lukewarm, and I can heat they ass back up real quick. Grams and Aunt Cynt came walking into the family room.

"What y'all got going on?" Grams asked, taking a seat.

"Nothing much. We're about to go to the mall with your grandsons."

"Oh ok. So, what y'all think about Cam and that Remi girl. I think they were more than just damn friends. I peeped how he looked at her and how nervous her ass got. She's a pretty girl and I like her. She seems like she would be a better fit than Slutville Saniya!" Grams looked like she was about to start some shit.

. . .

"Yeah, I think mom said that her and Cam went to school together, and she was his tutor," I stated.

"Yeah, I remember when he needed a tutor in college. Ju was his tutor for a while, but Cam wanted his ass fired expeditiously," Laila revealed, and we all fell out laughing

"Can you blame his ass? You never know what the hell Lil Einstein got going on. Cam called me and told me Ju built a house for them to meet in for their study sessions. And for a minute, I thought the nigga was showing love to his brother by moving near the campus. Cam ass was like nooooo Grams. It's all online. I said, ohhh hell to the nawl! Don't take yo' ass into cyber space with that nigga. He might be trying to traffic you and sell yo' ass on the black market. Ion trust smart niggas like that no mo'".

Give me a gun totin', dick draggin' the ground, drug lord any day of the week. These smart niggas might be done auctioned yo ass on the dark web forreal. Have your ass thinking he sending you to the mall on a shopping spree, and the next thing you know, your ass in Shanghai selling ass for Jai Kim an 'nem. Mmmmm mmmm! You can never be too careful, hunny." Grams shook her head and was serious as hell. I was laughing so damn hard my stomach was hurting. 'Cause I could see her telling Cam something like that. You would swear that he was her best friend, cause they were always on the phone gossiping. Cam, Ju, and Saniya came walking into the room. It's crazy how none of our spouses were able to come home with us on this trip. Myia's mom was really sick, so she was taking care of her.

"Y'all ready?" Ju asked.

"Yep, I can't wait to spend both of my brother's money." I

stood from my seat and rubbed my hands together for the damage I was about to do to their pockets.

"I know that's right." Laila high-fived me. We all headed out to the mall, and it was such a good feeling to hang with my sister and brothers. Cam and I had a talk about his girl, and I promised him that I would be a little nicer to her. It wasn't as if we just met the girl, she's been around for a while. We were on our way down to Fendi when I thought I saw Remi.

"Daddy Johnathan, can we have ice cream now!" The little girl asked her dad. Cam stopped walking when he saw them approaching. It took Remi a lil minute to notice us. The little girl took off running towards us.

"Daddy! Where have you been?" She excitedly screamed, wrapping her little arms around Cam's leg and that shit had us looking confused as fuck. All Cam could do was look from the little girl back to Remi.

"Where have you been? Didn't your parents teach you responsibility!" the little boy ran up and stomped his little feet down on Cam's foot.

"Mommy! Get your son! Don't touch my daddy, boy. What's wrong with you, we just got him and now you're trying to run him off already!" The little girl yelled, pushing her brother back away from Cam.

"Daddy! What the fuck is going on, Remi!"

"Yooo, dude! Don't you see these kids standing here!" The dude that was with Remi spoke up.

"Who the fuck are....Yooo ain't you the nigga from college? Nigga, I beat your ass back in school, and I'm a beast with it now, my nigga! It's best that you sit this one out, bruh!" Cam spat, getting into the dude's face. Remi stepped in between them to try to deescalate what was about to go down.

"Cam, please let me explain!" She tried to grab him.

"Get your fucking hands off my man, bitch." Saniya snapped.

"Oh, my fuckin' God! Ju, call mom & dad and tell them to get here now!" I blurted.

"These kids look identical to mom," Laila stated, and she was right. They both looked just like our mom, especially the little girl. I think the realization of what was happening hit everyone at the same damn time because we all looked at each other in disbelief.

"Cam, please!" She pleaded with my brother, but I could see that this was about to be some shit.

"Are these my fuckin' kids?!" He roared, getting into her face.

"Cam, can we talk in private?" She questioned, looking around.

"Remi, if these kids are my brother's. Why would you keep that shit from him?" I asked her, still confused as fuck.

"Fuck talking in private. We gone talk about this shit in public right now! All I wanna hear is if these kids are mine or not!" He gritted, pulling her closer to him.

"Mommy!" They cried with a face full of tears.

"Talk! The fuck!" Cam angrily spat.

"Bro, this isn't the time. We need to take this out of the mall," Ju said to him, but Cam wasn't trying to hear any of us. A crowd started to form, and when people realized that it was Cam, the cell phones came out and I'm sure they were recording. This shit was about to get messy, and I knew his publicist was going to have to put out so many damn fires.

"Are they my kids?!" When she looked up to face him with tears streaming down her face, we all knew what the answer would be.

"Hey, you two. I'm Ms. Laila. Let's go look at some toys right in that store. Is it alright if they go in the store with me?" She asked Remi. She nodded that it was alright, and the kids walked off with her. Thank God Laila stepped in to occupy them because this might go left real quick.

"Yes, they're yours! I'm so sorry, Cam," she cried.

"Fuckkkkkkkkk! You fuckin' bitch! How selfish could you fuckin' be! You let me go all of these years and not tell me about them!" He roared.

"Nigga, I told your ass about…" Before dude could get the rest of his sentence out, Cam went beast mode on his ass, beating the shit out of him in this mall. Our security attempted to stop him, but I held my hand up to stop them. Fuck that! I'mma let my brother get that aggression off on this nigga today.

"Oh, God! Cameron! Please stop, son." I heard my mother cry out, and I didn't even see them come up on us. Laila must have told them where we were. My dad gave me and Ju the side-eye, and he and Uncle Zelan rushed to pull Cam off ole dude.

"Nigga, you gone wish yo' ass never put hands on me, bitch!" The dude yelled and Cam broke free and was on his ass again. My dad and Uncle Zelan pulled him off him again, and this time security helped them.

"Bruh, it's best that you chill the fuck out! Let them handle their personal shit. This is not something you wanna get too deep into. You might walk into some shit you'll never walk out of," Uncle Zelan meant every word he said to the guy, and dude just backed up.

"Remi. I know this is a lot, but I need for you to come with us so that we can talk this through," I requested.

"No, I'm not going to sit here and let this dude call me out of my name and continuously disrespect me. I don't care who he is and what he's got. A nigga with money don't have me falling out all over the place. And please leave my friend alone. He has nothing to do with this." She went off, and I could understand her anger just a little.

"Girl, I understand that you're pissed, and under normal circumstances, you would have a valid reason to be. But you kept not one but two fuckin' babies from my brother! That lil' disrespect you catchin' right now, you gone have to eat that shit for little while," I told her.

"I'm not eating shit! Cam and his bitch need to know that I'm not that same girl from college. I'm sorry things happened this way, but I told him I was pregnant! That shit wasn't a secret to him. I did my job and went to him. He's the one that jumped to conclusions and formulated his own idea of what was going on and who the father of my kids was. When he said he was happy that he and I didn't mess up like that because he didn't need kids messing up his life, I gave him the freedom to be fucking free! I didn't want me and my kids out here messing up his life. Now he's out here disrespecting me on some fuck nigga shit, but it's all good." She looked over at Cam hysterically crying.

"Fuck nigga?! Respect?! I know your ass can't be serious right now? Bitch, did you give me any respect when you walked around for nine months carrying my fuckin' seeds in your stomach?! Did you give me any respect when you went to any of your doctor's appointments?! Did you give me any respect when you had your first labor pain?! Did you give me any respect when you were in full-blown labor?! Did you give me any respect when you celebrated their 1st,2nd, 3rd, 4th, or 5th fuckin' birthday?! Fuck no! You didn't give a nigga none of that, so don't talk to me about fuckin' showing you any type of respect!

You could've corrected me no matter what the fuck I said to

you that night. You could have simply said no my nigga I'm pregnant by you! The fuck is you saying! You're sitting there trying to make yourself feel better about the FUCK SHIT you did. I'm not trying to hear any of that bullshit from you! Now I've missed years of their life, all because yo' ass was in your feelings. Stay the fuck away from me because all I feel right now is me wrapping my fuckin' hands around your neck!" He roared.

"Cameron! What the hell are you doing, son! No matter what's going on, you're a Kassom, and this is not how we act! Stop talking to her like that! We need to figure out what's going on, so that we can get to the bottom of all this," Mom told him.

"Mom, I love you; please don't do that! We know what's going on; she got pregnant by me and hid that she had my kids. This girl could have told me about them, yet she got them out here calling this pussy ass nigga daddy like all is right in the fuckin' world. Every time they open their mouth to call that nigga daddy, I'm fuckin' his pussy ass up! I put that on everything I love. You better unteach them everything you taught them about that nigga cause it's on sight!" he roared, trying to charge at the dude again.

"I'm sorry!" Remi cried out.

"Fuck your sorry! Urrggggggggghhhhhhhhh! This is some fuckin' bullshit, man!" He roared as the tears fell from his eyes. Now, this shit was just heartbreaking because they were both broken over this. My mom and I were both in tears as well. It was more to Cam and Remi's story, and I'm sure we were about to find out just how deep this shit went. Mall security was here, and of course, dad's security team was trying to put out the fire.

"Son, let's go outside. We can't be in here causing a scene," my dad stated. Cam turned to walk out with our dad and Uncle

Z. We all followed them out, but we kind of kept our distance so that dad and Uncle Zelan could talk to Cam.

"I can't believe he even fucked you!" Saniya spat.

"Girl, shut the fuck up!" Remi jumped in her face, and her friend pulled her to the side to talk to her. The kids were holding on tight to their mom's hand.

"My God, their resemblance to me is amazing. They're so beautiful! My baby has babies that we knew nothing about." My mom cried, and I don't think anything could have prepared this family for something like this.

Chapter Nine

REMI

I couldn't believe this nigga was out here really going off on me like that. I get it, he's pissed, but he knew what it was back then. He knew exactly what the hell he said, and now we're here with it. I didn't want to be dishonest with my kids because I knew one day they would ask about their dad. I knew it wasn't right because there were days that they cried for him. They needed their father's love, and I tried to love them enough as their mother and for their father.

My heart was crushed seeing the hurt in his eyes. I feared that this day would happen, and there was no way to ever prepare for it. I never expected Cam to call me out of my name like that though. He's right. Maybe I should have told him. I just didn't want to be the reason things didn't work out for him.

"I think we need to get the kids home," Johnathan spoke, and I agreed with him. I knew he was beyond pissed. Johnathan's hate for Cam was deep but he knew he could never disrespect Cam. He was my children's father, and that was that. However,

I'm not going to let Cam disrespect my best friend either. The kids have seen enough, and I feel bad for allowing them to see me and their dad fighting. I've never put them in an uncomfortable situation. Just as we were about to walk away, Cam's dad walked over to me.

"Are you alright?" He asked with a concerned expression.

"I'm fine, but my kids are a little shaken. They have never been in a situation like this. I don't cause drama, nor have I ever been in any drama," I replied.

"Hmmm, that's interesting. This entire situation is full of drama. Cam is in a rage, and to be honest, he has somewhat of a right to be. The damage is done. Now we have to figure out how to fix it all. I would like to apologize for the way he spoke to you. I hope that you both will calm down and talk this out for the sake of the children. If at all possible, can you come back to the house so that we can properly meet them?" he asked.

"Sir, with all due respect, they need to get home. Maybe y'all can set an appointment to talk at a later time. Your son has done enough damage for one day. He needs to be worried about playing in that game and me pressing charges on his ass. I suggest y'all lawyer up," Jonathan spat and I think he should have just shut the hell up.

"Lawyer up?! Nigga, let me let you in on a lil' secret. I don't have to get ready when I stay ready. That dude to the left of you that's on the phone is the head of my legal team. Don't ever get shit fucked up. I have enough lawyers on my team to start my own bar association. I think the best thing for you to do is to just stop talking. Your fuck nigga threats will never make any of the Kassom family jump. This family stands together every time. Trust me if you're coming for one of us, that will be the biggest mistake you'll ever make in your life.

Oh, one more thing, don't let any of this professionalism fool you. I will kill you before you can suck in your next breath of fuckin' air! Don't ever come for my children! Pussy ass nigga! Remi, I hope you and the kids will consider coming back with us. Cameron needs to meet his children, and they need to properly meet their father. We have a security detail for you, and your truck is number three." He smiled, pointing in the direction of the truck. That's when I realized it was so many trucks and security out here. I was still trying to pick my mouth up off the ground because he just read Johnathan to fucking filth.

"Johnathan, I'm going with them. This is a conversation that I have to have with him. He deserves to spend time with them and get to know his kids. I appreciate and love you so much for protecting us, but I got it from here." I kissed his cheek.

"Mommy, I don't want to go with them. I want to go with daddy Johnathan." Kaleb pouted. The moment he called Johnathan daddy, my heart started beating fast. Both Johnathan and I were looking around for Cam.

"On sight, my nigga!" Cameron gritted, moving towards us.

"Cameron, let's go!" His uncle yelled, pulling him away. Johnathan just walked off. He didn't even say goodbye to the kids.

I walked over to the truck with the kids, and we all got in, and they pulled off. My cell phone was ringing, and I grabbed it because I'm sure Jonathan had called Zori. To my surprise, it was my cousin Shanae.

"Hey, cousin. Is everything alright?" I asked her.

"Girl, we good over here. Me and your mama calling to check on yo' ass! I was scrolling on IG while my Friday nigga was trying to climb this tree of sexiness and threw his little ass off when I saw you in the damn Shaderoom going toe to toe with that sexy ass Cam! Girl, you done fucked around and hid that nigga chirren, so them lil exotic looking kids of yours is his?" She asked, and all I could do was shake my head because I knew she was about to act up.

"Yes, they're his kids."

"Wheeewww! Girl, why you hide them kids like that? The whole time yo' ass was home struggling, and you could've been living in luxury eating crab legs, lobster, and shit. I would've said them lil fish eggs, but hood black people don't eat that shit. It be them uppity ass black people that finally made it out the hood, that try that nasty shit. Now that your value as baby mama done went up, don't be eating that nasty shit you still hood black. That's what the fuck I'm talking 'bout. It's rich nigga Friday for my cousin!

Chile, it looks like it's gone take him a few months to calm down before y'all can go around him. He looked like he was ready to tear that damn mall down, boo! The Shaderoom and other gossip blogs got y'all out here looking bad. I know these hoes 'bout to blast off on you in these comments, and I'mma be right there cussin' these ugly-faced hoes out. Cause the fuck they thought we was. Don't come for my cousin on any level, hoe. We were doing a nigga check foe we claimed that rich nigga. He made it, and now he belongs to us. He dem babies pappy!" She laughed, and I was trying to hold in my laughter, but this girl was crazy.

"I'm on my way to talk to him, and his family so I will call you when I get home," I told her.

"Hell nawl, cuz! Girl, you better not take your ass over there. What if them people kill yo' ass for hiding them, kids? Rich people rich for a reason, all it takes is money to hide a body. Do you even know his family like that? You might have fucked your way into the wrong muthafuckin' family. Just cause they look good on the outside, them muthafuckas could be batshit crazy on the inside. I hope your ass is strapped, and if they start looking at yo' ass funny, they 'bout to kill you, sis. I hate you got yourself into this mess. I just pray to God and his homies that you didn't try the wrong nigga." Shan ass was crazy.

"They are not like that, the Kassom family is very nice and a well-known prominent family." We talked for a few minutes, and I told her and my mom I would call them back later, because we were pulling into the gates of the Kassom estate.

"Wooowww! Mommy, this is a big houseeeee!" Kammy yelled excitedly. Kaleb was still pouting, and I think it was going to take a little more time with him.

Once the cars came to a stop, the driver got out to help me and the kids out of the car. My eyes connected with Cam's and all I could see is the level of pain he was going through. He stood by the door waiting for me and the kids, and his fiancée made sure she stood right next to him. We all walked into the family room, and the rest of the family was sitting around drinking and laughing.

"Ciera, why these lil kids look like you?" Ms. Laila asked, getting up from her seat.

"Hi, I'm Kamryn Blake. Are you related to my daddy?" Kamryn asked her.

"Well, that depends, we can't be going around here claiming other people's kids. Who yo' daddy?" She asked Kammy.

"His name is Camron Kassom, he's the best quarterback in the NFL, and he's set the record for the highest passes in the league. I have his Jersey at my mommy's house. I'm going to get him to sign it just in case he has to go away and I never see him again." She smiled, and Cam walked out of the room. The next thing we heard was glass shattering and him cursing. His parents ran out of the room, and I knew it was time that I had a talk with him.

"Hey, you two, go sit on the couch, and I'll be right back." I walked into the kitchen, and Saniya got closer to him.

"Saniya, they need to talk. I think we should give them some privacy," Ciera suggested, and this bitch didn't budge.

"I'm not going anywhere. She can explain why she kept these so-called babies of his away. You need to know we're getting a DNA test done. My man ain't gone be out here…"

"Leave the kitchen, Niya!" Cam yelled, cutting her off, and she stormed out of the kitchen.

"Cameron, you need to get that girl in check before I punch her in her shit." His mom left out of the kitchen, mad as hell. For a minute, he just stared at me, and I felt so damn uncomfortable to the point I started playing with my damn hands.

"Remi, why would you not tell me? You had a chance to correct me. Please don't give me that lame-ass excuse on some you said you wasn't ready bullshit! You were pregnant with my kids, Remi! I'm rich now, Remi, and I was rich back then. What the fuck could you have possibly messed up? We would have worked it out. All you had to do was say that you were pregnant by me."

"I'm so sorry, Cam. I'm truly sorry that I didn't come right out and say it. I wasn't trying to stop what you had going on. I really wanted to see you excel in your career. I never set out to hurt you," I cried.

"You only thought about your feelings and what you thought was right! You never gave me chance. You never allowed me to make any decisions for my life, or theirs. How old are they?" He asked.

"They're five; their birthdays are on June 12th." The more we talked, the more messed up I felt.

"Unbelievable, that's my dad's birthday. You had me miss five years of their life. I missed so many damn moments. When you were pregnant, doctor visits so I could hear their heartbeats, when you found out that you were having twins, I missed their first everything!" he angrily spat, and I was in tears. I tried to hug him, and he stepped away from me.

"Don't fucking do that!" he roared.

"Cam, I don't know what else to do or say," I cried.

"There ain't shit you can do or say. It's fucked up on so many levels. I would like to talk to them. My lil baby damn near knows everything about me. The fuck!" He sighed, sitting down at the bar. He was displaying an array of emotions- Anger, disappointment, hurt, shock, defeat, and one that I'd never seen from Cam in all of my time of knowing him, *fear*.

"I know I was wrong, but I made sure our children knew you loved them even though they'd never met you. They formed their own connection with you through your interviews, games, and photos. I know saying this can't take away your hurt, but you aren't a stranger to them. Kaleb is just in his feelings, but he loves you." I was trying my best to plead my case, but the shit wasn't working. He had to know; I wasn't just some sneaky ass bitter woman that was hiding his kids away from him. I did what I felt was right at the time to Protect Cam and his future. I didn't expect for this to go on as long as it did but then again, I didn't expect for us to run into the Kassom family either. Things were just all bad and no matter how a person looked at this situation, I looked like the bad person.

"I want them tested as soon as possible!" He stood from the

chair and walked out of the kitchen. Like what was happening now. Was he done talking to me?

Just as I was about to walk out of the kitchen, Saniya walked in. "Let me let you in on a little secret, bitch! Cameron will never leave me for you and those kids. So, if you think for one second that you're going to get him, over my dead body!" She gritted.

"I don't want your man but suit yourself because you got one more time to speak on me or my kids, and I'mma dog walk your ass." I walked out of the kitchen. I headed back to the family room to check on my kids, and Kammy was talking to Mr. Juelz.

"So, is it true are you my daddy's dad?" She asked him.

"Yes, that's true." He smiled down at her.

"Soooo, that would make you, my Papa? Are you rich like my daddy? Is this your big house?" She inquired.

"Yes, this house belongs to me and your grandmother." The way Kammy looked over at her grandma and smiled made me smile.

"That's cool! Papa, we like ice cream, and if you have a lot of money, can you buy an ice cream store for me and Kaleb? I want to eat ice cream whenever we want because waiting for mom to take us could be days." She rolled her eyes, and everyone laughed at her antics.

"I will discuss it with your dad and figure it out, alright?" Juelz looked over at Cam, and he nodded at his dad. Cam walked over and bent down to talk to the kids.

"Can I talk to you guys for a minute? I promise to be good." Both of the kids went with him, and I didn't follow them because the three of them needed this time alone.

CAM

I was ready to fuckin' tear this house up! I can't believe this shit was happening. She had so much time to tell me about being pregnant. Why the fuck would she do some shit like that to me! That shit she's talking is some straight bullshit. She could have yelled that shit out. Fuck what the hell I was talking about that night in the pizza shop. She could have stopped my ass mid-sentence and *say nah, Cam, I'm pregnant by you. Not the flaky nigga.* That would have been a game-changer for all of us. But knowing would have allowed us to work this shit out together. She wouldn't have had to drop out of school. I know my dad would have helped us find an alternative for her. This shit is fuckin' crazy. I was sitting here with Kamryn and Kaleb, and we were all just quiet, just staring at each other. It's so fucked up I don't even know what to say to them.

"Dad, this is kind of weird. You have to say something to us. Are you nervous? Do you want me to hold your hand?" The look on her little face was an expression that instantly melted my heart for her. Those gray eyes reminded me of her mother and my mother, but I can believe how much she looks like my mom. She was my mom inside of a little body. I swear we have never seen anything like this.

"He doesn't have anything to say because he's going to leave us again," Kaleb spat with so much anger in his tiny chest. I'm so amazed at how well-spoken, and how incredibly smart they are. I shouldn't be shocked because their mother is a damn genius with it. Not to mention my brother Ju. My lil baby girl got all of that feistiness from my side of the family for sure.

"Lil man, I wouldn't have left you if I knew that I was having you. Me not being a part of your life is because I didn't know you existed. I promise you both I would've been there with your mother every step of the way." I pulled him up from his seat because it seemed that he needed me to wrap my arms around him. There is nothing like having the love of your father. When a child feels like he doesn't have that, it could be hard on him and for him. I never want that for my lil man. I know all too well how that shit could fuck with your mental. There were many times where I felt like I needed that hug from my dad and never got it. I knew without a doubt that he loved me, he just didn't show it through affection as much with me. I pulled away from him so that I could make a promise to him, and his little face was full of tears.

"Come here, baby." I held my hand out for Kamryn to come over with us.

"I wanna make a promise to you both now that I know I have you. I promise that you both have me for life. I know you both know that play football. I don't live here in New York; I live in Atlanta, so I will have to leave soon because I have a game. Just know that you will never be without me. I'm going to always be a part of your life. I love you both." I kissed the both of them on top of their heads, and Kaleb held onto me a little tighter.

"I love you, lil guy. And I got you from this moment on." I smiled down at him.

"That doesn't mean he loves you more, cry baby. It just means he thinks you need extra attention. But you call me dumb; I think you're a little soft." His sister licked her tongue and rolled her eyes at him.

"You're still dumb." He licked his tongue back at her.

"Heyyy, we don't do that. You're supposed to love and protect your little sister. Andd Kam…"

"Hold on, pop! You just got here; it's too soon," Kamryn said, cutting me off in her lil squeaky voice, and my damn mouth was hanging the hell open. *Did this little girl just check me, when I was only trying to take up for her?* I mean, I was going to get her little butt next for talking her brother like that, but I guess she got me first. I had to laugh because I just know she's going to have all the men in this family wrapped around her entire hand, especially her daddy. I have never in my life felt love like I have in my heart for them right now. That shit took over my heart instantly! I talked to them for a little while longer, and then we joined the family back in the family room. Their mom was sitting on the couch talking to Laila, and Kari and Saniya was sitting across the room with hatred written all over her face as she openly stared at Remi.

"Son, I know you're upset, but I need you to remain calm and try to talk to her respectfully because what we don't need is her running off with the kids. I just think we all need to take a minute to relax. The kids have seen so much today, and from what she's told your dad, this doesn't happen around them. They have never seen her in any altercations. Now they're looking at you act out, screaming, and yelling at their mom. Little Kaleb hasn't said much since he's been here. The only person he's talking to is JuJu, and that's because Ju said he was in his camp," Mom revealed.

"She's right, grandson. You can't be calling these hoes out they name like that in front of these kids 'cause what if she a reformed hoe, and the kids didn't know they mammy was a hoe. Now that hoe you 'bout to marry. Well, she just a hoe and ain't shit reformed about her ass! If I never told you this, grandson, just know ion like that hoe! Me and your uncle Zelan tried to teach you the game, 'cause we knew you were raised up a privileged kid. We should have worked a lil' harder, 'cause now you got this chick that's ready to take you for everything you got! I bet if you mention prenup, her ass gone be ready to fight up in here! You see that chile with them kids, she didn't give a damn about your money. Her ass could have rocked you for child support for them babies and been living her best life." Grams laughed. I looked over at the kids playing and talking with my dad, and mom as their mom watched on with a smile.

"Papa, do the security people make sure you're ok?" Kamryn asked him.

"Yes, they make sure that we're all ok," Dad responded.

"I think I need security and so does Kaleb because he can't have my security guy. Do you have a pretty girl to security me and she can play with my dolls? Grandma, do you wanna play with my dolls?" She looked over at my mom.

"Yes, baby. I would love to play with your dolls." Mom smiled at her.

"Yeah, she a Kassom 'cause that lil' thang bossy and knows what she wants." Grams laughed, and we all agreed with her.

"She's been that way since she was three years old." Remi shook her head, and I smiled at the thought of my babies when they were younger. I really wished that I was there with them to see all phases of their growing up.

"Babe, are you alright?" Saniya asked, wrapping her arms around me.

"I'm good. I need you to watch how you speak to my mom. That's going to be the last time I talk to you about her. The situation I have with my kids is sensitive, and I need you to stay out of it. I will deal with Remi; don't say anything to her." She was pissing me off with the shit she's been saying.

"I'm your fiancee, I have a right to say what I need to say to her. You're calling them your kids and you haven't taking the first DNA test. They could be anybody's kids. What the fuck is wrong with you?" She yelled, which caused everyone to turn their attention to us. I pulled her out of the room to address her.

"You don't tell me what I should and shouldn't do. I'm a grown ass man, and those babies are mine! Let me tell you this shit right now. Even if a blood test is done and it comes back that they are not mine, I'm fuckin' invested in them, so they still gone be mine! If you can't rock with that shit, then I guess we got a problem. I love you, and nothing is going to stop me from loving you. But you better get your shit together because I'm not putting up with all of this extra bullshit. Now I know you feel some type of way about the way some of my family is treating you, and I will deal with them," I told her.

"Who his ass talking 'bout dealing with? He gone deal with is the bird brain hoe he talkin' too! I done told yo' ass once, these hoes ain't loyal, nigga! Talkin 'bout dealing with us. Nigga, we the assassin nine, 'round here ain't nobody dealing with us!" Grams fussed. I knew I would have to see her about what I said. Saniya walked off heading towards the elevator mad as hell.

"Cam, I think it's time for me to get the kids home and in

bed. They've had a long day and they're hungry and tired." Remi walked out into the hall.

"Can y'all stay the night here? I want to spend a little more time with them." I looked over at her.

"We don't have a change of clothes with us, and I think it's best that we go home. I can bring them back in the morning so that they can hang out with you and maybe stay the night tomorrow night with you." It was hard to agree to that because I really didn't want them to leave.

"Ok, but I'm going with you. I wanna help get them ready for bed." I was still pissed with her, but I was trying to do what my mom said and calm down a little.

"Alright." She smiled and walked back into the room to get the kids together. The kids said goodbye to the family.

"Ok, kiddos, we have to go home. It's way past your dinner time, and then you have to get ready for bed." Remi seemed like she took good care of them. We got the kids together and headed out to the car and the security that my dad assigned to them.

"Cam, are they seriously going with us?" Remi questioned.

"Yes, you have my babies, and they need to be secured at all times. My dad assigned them to you and the kids at the mall. Until we have things figured out, I need to make sure y'all are safe." I made sure they were all inside and then got inside the truck.

"Cam, I understand wanting the kids safe, but I don't think it's necessary. I don't want our lives to change. We were comfortable the way we were." She looked over at me once we got comfortable in the car.

"Your life changed the moment I found out you had my kids. There isn't and will never be a negotiation stage about their safety." She turned to look out the window without responding to what I said, and to be honest, that shit didn't bother me one bit. Yeah, we're definitely gonna have to lay down some rules. I get that she's been doing shit her way since they were born, but that's before I knew they were mine. People know I have kids since we had that shit blasted on the internet, and I'm not playing any of that shit. I will go to war behind them, and what I can't handle by my fuckin' self, I got a squad of Kassom goons that will damn sure show up and drop yo' ass.

My mom and dad tried to shelter me from a lot of shit, but my sister did what she had to do to get and keep me ready. I'm a Kassom, and I bust my muthafuckin' guns like one. And now that I have them, we're definitely gonna have to figure out these living arrangements. I'm not trying to be away from them.

Chapter Eleven

REMI

I'm glad Cam calmed down enough to talk to me respectfully. Because the way he was calling me out my name really had me ready to fight. I hated getting confrontational and all the name-calling. He said that he was going back to Atlanta in a couple of days, and now he doesn't want to leave the kids.

"Mommy, is daddy still mad at you?" Kammy asked.

"No, baby. He's better now."

"If he's still mad, you have to say sorry, mom. Me and Kaleb talked, and we want him to stay with us," she stated.

"Your dad and I have to work through some things, but he's not going to leave you and Kaleb. He's gonna have to leave to play football, and when he's done, he will come back to see you and your brother." I leaned down to hug her.

"Mommy, I hope daddy lives with us, and we can have a wedding and marry daddy." She clapped her hands excitedly. Just as I was about to respond, Cam walked into the room.

"Is Kaleb all settled?" I questioned, trying to change the subject.

"Yeah, he's tired. After we had our little talk, and I reassured him that I got him from here on out, it didn't take him long to fall asleep. I see this little beauty is still full of energy." He leaned down to tickle her.

"Daddy, me, you, mommy, and Kaleb is getting married. We're going to be so pretty, and you have to take me to get a pretty dress in Bora Bora, daddy." Kammy had the biggest smile spread across her face, but I was so damn embarrassed. My baby girl is so adorable, and her imagination is out of this world. Like where the hell did she get Bora Bora from? And who told her we were getting married?

"Kammy, daddy is already en...." Before I could get the rest of my sentence out, Cam cut me off.

"Nah, that's a conversation for another day." He had this uneasy look on his face, but I didn't want my baby having big dreams thinking that we were all going to be this one big happy family, because we weren't. One thing I didn't do is lie to my kids and fill their heads with bullshit.

"Baby, it's time to go to close your eyes and get some sleep." I leaned down to kiss her goodnight, and so did her dad. It has been a long stressful day, and I need a drink or three, and a long hot shower.

"I'm going to help mommy make banana pancakes, daddy, for breakfast," Kammy said to him.

"Ok, baby. I can't wait to taste them." I looked over at Cam in disbelief for agreeing to be here for breakfast. I turned her light off and made sure her night light was on. Cam and I went out into the living room and took a seat.

"I'm still taken back by how things have changed with you,

from your looks to the way you talk now. When did you move to New York, though? I thought you went home to South Carolina when you left school." He looked over at me, and all I saw was pain and confusion.

"Zori helped me get a job at the network, and the kids and I have been here for a little over four years now. Zori is really a good friend, and I really hate that the interview with you was snatched from under her because we're both trying to make a name for ourselves. I hope she's not mad with me because of the stunt you pulled. With all that's happened today, I haven't heard from her not one time, and I've even called her." Cam didn't seem to have any emotions about what I just said to him.

"I get it, she's your friend, and y'all look out for one another. I wanted you to do the interview, and that's what it was gone be, lil baby. I'm not trying to take food from nobody's table, or money out of their pockets. I will figure something out in regard to Zori and the network if that makes you feel better." He shrugged.

"Would you like something to drink?" I asked, deciding to change the subject.

"I'm good. Remi, I need you to sit down and talk to me, baby girl 'cause I really need some answers. I don't get any of this shit. Why didn't you just tell me, even if it was later down the road? Would you have even told me if we hadn't run into y'all at the mall? Why leave me in the fuckin' dark like that? We've known one another long enough to know I wouldn't have left you hanging, lil mama. When you didn't have money in school, I'm the one that always made sure your pockets were on full." He sighed, rubbing his hands over his face.

"I was afraid. I truly didn't want to interfere with your career.

I knew how much playing football meant to you. I wanted you to live out your dreams," I responded.

"Yet your dreams were shattered by two words *you're pregnant!* Make that make sense for me, Remi. How do you allow me to live my shit out, but you had to drop out of school to raise my kids? Nah, don't ever in your life think for me again. I would have made sure that we both lived out our dreams and took care of our babies. You can't make decisions like that for me? Especially about my kids. All of my decisions at that point would have been about them," he said to me, and I felt so bad.

"Cam, I'm truly sorry. There isn't anything I can do to change the decisions I made. Even though I'm sorry for the way things played out and how it affected you and the kids. But my love for you in my mind wanted you to make it without any inter-ference from me. If you asked me right now would I do it again, the answer would be yes." The way he looked at me scared the shit out of me, but I'm standing on what I said.

"You know what? I'm gone head out before I say some shit to hurt your feelings. I think enough pain has been caused on both sides today. I'm coming to eat breakfast here in the morning with my kids, and then I would like to take them back to my parent's house to spend some time with them before I head back to Atlanta. I gotta practice before my game on Sunday."

"That's fine. They normally wake up around 8:30 each day." I gave a half smile because hearing that he was mad at me again was hurtful.

"Cool." Is all he said and headed for the door.

"Cam, wait." I grabbed his arm before he could walk out of the door.

"It's best that you don't touch me!" I can't believe that he was acting this way when I was only thinking about him.

"Cam, please." I tried grabbing him again and I guess that was a trigger for him because he hemmed me against the wall.

"Don't fuckin' touch me!" the way he stared into my eyes hurt me because all I saw was disappointment. His lips were inches from mine, and I could feel the heat from his breath tickling my lips. His stare intensified, and it seemed as if he moved a little closer to me because if I made one wrong move, my lips would be on his. The temperature in my body began to rise, and lord knows this wasn't the time for me to fall weak. We were ready to rip each other's heads off ten hours ago. I've loved this man since the day I started tutoring him. Never in a million years did I think he would sleep with me and ultimately I would have his children. The way my body was reacting to him being this close to me, the moment I moved to break free from him, was the moment my lips touched his. He hungrily sucked my lips into his mouth, and there was nothing I could do in that moment. I didn't want to be weak for him, but damn, I've loved this man for years. He pulled away from me as I stood there panting with a soaking wet pussy.

He shook his head, turning to walk out without saying anything else to me. Like what the hell was that? I lowkey thought he was about to fuck me, and I swear I would have let him. That's how bad I want him, and I know it would be wrong because he's with Saniya. But I don't like that girl and damn sure don't give a damn about her feelings. I stormed off into my bedroom mad as hell because I was now hot, and fucking bothered.

I grabbed my rose from the drawer beside my bed and went into the bathroom for a shower. This rose will have your ass stroking out, dying, and coming back to life a new woman. I don't know how many of these damn things I done burned out,

I've bought so many of them I probably need stock in the damn company. After I handled my business, I showered and crawled into bed with Cam on my mind as I drifted off to sleep.

The doorbell sounding off jolted me out of my sleep. Looking over at the clock, it was a little after seven in the morning. I jumped up to answer the door before the doorbell went off again. I know it may sound crazy, but I hate when my kid's sleep is disturbed. It's bad enough I wake them up extra early for school during the week, but on the weekends, it's their time, and I let them sleep as long as they want to. Snatching the door opened, I got the surprise of my life, and for some reason, I felt so relieved to see them.

"What are y'all doing here?" I asked excitedly, pulling my mom and cousin into a hug.

"Girl, from the look of things on them people's social media platforms, you needed us. I been on these damn fourteen hundred 'leven posts from Twitter to muthafuckin' Instagram fighting for my lil cousin's honor and yo' ass up in this bitch sleeping like Sleeping Beauty done woke up and poof issa golden dick rich nigga's baby mama round this bitch! Bihhh, it's war out here in these muthafuckin' streets. These lil' pretty boy Cam bitches want yo' head on a muthafuckin' platter for breakfast, lunch, and dinner for the way you did that boy. And we not gone even talk about all the fuckin' press surrounding the building, lil baby." I ran out on my patio to see what the fuck Shan was talking about, and I damn near bust my ass getting back inside my apartment when they spotted me.

"Chile, one of yo' titties about to be on Mediatakeout! Didn't

I just tell yo' ass they was down there and yet you still take yo' half-naked ass out there to go look?" Shan shook her head, plopping down on the couch.

"Baby, are you alright? I tried to call you a few times last night when Shan showed me all that was going on. They said that boy was already super-rich, his daddy is that multi-billionaire that own all of them banks. Why didn't you tell me, Remi? You wouldn't have had to struggle with them the way you did." My mom sighed, and I know she might not understand my why. But who and what Cam has isn't my concern. He had dreams outside of what his parents had, and I wanted his dreams to be his reality. People can say whatever they want to about me. Just as long as they don't talk down on my babies, we're good.

"Mom, I had my reasons for not telling anyone who their father was, and I also had my reasons for not disturbing his life. If that's a problem for you, I'll be more than happy to pay you back anything you've ever done for me during that time." I know I shouldn't have come off like that with her. I knew back then if people found out I was pregnant by him, the first thing they would say is to go after his money. Or that money was the only thing I wanted from him.

"I'm sorry, mom. I never meant to come off mean to you. I just felt as if my decisions on not saying who their father was wasn't something I wanted to share with anyone." I hugged my mom because I never wanted her to feel disrespected by me. My phone and doorbell was going off, and I answered the door without thinking about what I had on.

"Fuck!" He muttered under his breath.

"I need for you to put some clothes on; my parents are coming down the hall." Is all he had to say because my ass took off running. I could hear my cousin in a fit of laughter and left it up to them to introduce themselves. I rushed to take care of my hygiene, and I threw on a pair of tights, t-shirt and slid on my Fendi slides. Cam and his parents were talking to my mom and cousin when I walked back out into the living room.

"Good morning, Remi. I hope you don't mind us coming over with Cam. With all that went on yesterday, we didn't have a chance to speak to you in private." Ciera smiled.

"I think we need to discuss what's going on outside and the possibilities of you moving out of here for a while," Mr. Kassom stated, and I had to look at him as if he was a lil crazy because what in the hell is he talking about. I'm not moving anywhere.

"What! Who said I was moving? I'm confused? I'm not uprooting my kids just because it's public knowledge that Cam's their father," I said to him, and I guess that didn't sit well with them. Just because they had money, that shit didn't move me.

"We're going to do whatever we need to do to protect them and you because you're their mother. You may think things can go back to normal, but I'm here to tell you your days of normalcy is over. You waking up this morning with every media network from news reporters, newspapers, magazines, and blogs downstairs should've been your first warning. Your picture plastered all over the internet should've been your second. Remi, we're not here to make your life harder, and trust me, I hate that things have to change like this for you, but we can't have our grandchildren sitting out in the open like this. Cam needs to know that they're protected and safe, and as their grandparents, my wife and I feel the same way," Mr. Kassom stated.

"Remi, my dad's publicist is downstairs trying to handle the media attention all of this has gotten. I don't know how they got your address so fast, but they have it, and I need you to get the kids together and relocate for a little while. You can come with me to Atlanta or stay with my parents, but y'all can't stay here." I was already in disagreement with Cam. I hope he didn't think he was about to turn our lives upside down because that shit wasn't happening.

"Cam, I'm sorry, but I'm not going anywhere. I have taken care of my kids for the past five years, and I'm not moving, nor am I changing the way we live."

"Daddyyyy! Na-Na!" Kammy screamed excitedly when she saw her dad and my mom.

"Na-Na! We found our daddy, and I got my other Grandma, Grandma, and she looks just like me! Looook, there is my Grandma and Papa!" Kammy pointed, and she took off running into Mr. Kassom's arms and Kaleb ran into his dad's. Ever since Kaleb and his dad had their one-on-one talk, he's warmed up to his dad.

"Cousin, I know you might be a lil' pissed, but they're right. You have a different life now, and things are changing. You don't have kids by some regular ass Joe ass nigga. That man is loved all over this country and is getting ready to play in one of the most important games of his career. You know I will never tell you anything wrong. You have to figure this out for the sake of those babies. Besides, that fine ass daddy can tell me what to do any day of the week! Looking like a fine, aged, established, you can't fuck with me, I'm that nigga, niggas wanna be, I got my rich ass shit together type of nigga. Chile, I bet he can slang dick with the best of 'em. He look like he got a dragon he draggin'. That's probably why you so strung out on the Jr. cause Sr. probably taught his ass errrthang! Let me go sit down and stop lusting on good sis man." Shan crazy-ass damn sure knew how to lighten my mood. I know I might be wrong for not working with them, but these were my kids.

"Remi, can we talk for a second?" Ms. Ciera asked, walking into the kitchen.

"Sure." I crossed my arms over my chest, waiting on her to start talking. It almost seemed as if it was me against all of them, and now my guard was up.

"I don't want you to think that we're here to pressure you into anything. You have to understand that we're all shocked that Cameron has kids that we knew nothing about. It was wrong of you to keep them away from him. There isn't anything we can do about the past; we have to move forward. I want what's best for my grandbabies, and everything we're suggesting is for them. I'm going to let you in on a secret. My husband didn't know about me being pregnant at first. I was acting off of emotions just like you did, and I was determined to live my life with my babies without him. So, trust me I understand that emotions can lead you into making decisions you might later regret.

Cam has missed five impressionable years with his kids. Just work with him, and I know you both can make this work. Juelz and I are going to head home. Maybe you and your family can come over and hang out with us for our family dinner later today. Cam is leaving to go back to Atlanta tomorrow, and I know he wants to spend as much time with his children as possible. He's going through a lot of emotions right now, and as his mother, I'm asking you to work through this with him," she requested. When I glanced in his direction, our eyes connected as he talked with my cousin and mom. Cam helped me get the kids dressed, and we all went headed to the Kassom estate.

Chapter Twelve

JUELZ

All of our family and friends were here to celebrate with Cam before he went back to Atlanta to play in the last playoff game that could possibly send him to the super bowl. Gabe & Gia, Melanie & Mano, Laila & Nigel, Truth & Shy, and even Jah had made it here to be a part of the festivities. Hearing that Cam had kids had me ready to choke his ass. I had to remember that he was grown and could have a hundred kids if he wanted to have them. I needed to talk to him because this boy was going to burn a damn hole in Ms. Remi. I know he's pissed about her keeping his kids away from him, so it isn't much I could say. I swear had Ci kept my kids away from me for five years, I know I would have acted a damn fool. I've decided to let him handle his business as he sees fit, just as long as he doesn't hurt her. Watching my wife as she talked and laughed with our kids, had my heart full. Sometimes I think back on when I met Ciera and can't believe the beautiful life we've created for our children and grandchildren.

"How are you feeling about our boy? This could be a big distraction for him, and I'm praying that he does alright." Zelan was right. I didn't think about how this was going to affect him in the big game.

"He has to have his head in the game, and I know not having them with him is going to throw him off. I know they can't move in with him when he has Saniya there. She's already giving him hell about Remi, and the kids," I told him.

"She would be on the other side of the door over my kids. I don't play about that shit. It's something up with that chick. Have you looked into her? Just because she's been with Cam since college doesn't mean shit." Zelan didn't trust anybody.

"Yeah, she's been investigated. She has some brothers in the streets of New Orleans, but they're not moving enough weight to make any noise down there. I don't think she even claims them." I turned to look on at my wife and kids and smiled. Ciera was just as beautiful as she was the day I met her. My heart was full watching my children and grandchildren. Cam, Ju, Laila, and Kari walked inside the house.

"Is everything alright?" I asked my wife, walking up to her, pulling her into my arms, and kissing her lips.

"Yes, they're trying to cheer their brother up. Now that he has them, he doesn't want to leave them, and Saniya isn't making things easier for him. She wants a DNA test before Cam just allows Remi and her kids into their lives. Juelz, I would be in agreeance with her if some girl just came out and said Cam got her pregnant. But this girl has been hiding these kids from him for years. She's been following his career and teaching these babies about their dad. They know everything about Cameron. Then there's the fact that they look just like me, and I feel it in my heart that they belong to us. Those are my grandchildren,

85

and I don't want them to be tested to prove something we already know." One thing my wife would go to war about is her children and grandchildren. So, if the queen said they belong to her bloodline, that's what it is.

"Oh, and Juelz, my son is stressed. I need for you to help him through this. If it takes buying her home in Atlanta so that the kids are close, we need to do that. If she insists on staying here, give her one of the homes in one of our developments." She kissed my lips and walked over to Grams.

"Did you lay it on thick cause I need my grandson right for this damn game? Me and Zelan got a lot of money riding on his ass," Grams said.

"I know that's right." Gabe high-fived her and they all fell out laughing. One of these days, my wife was going to get a no from me, and that shit is going to shock the world. Walking into the house, I could hear the kids talking.

"So, you kissed her?" I heard Kari question.

"Yeah, and to be honest, that shit brought back all the feelings I had for her. To be honest, Remi and I have only been together once, and that one time was enough. I'm just so fuckin' pissed that she did this shit to me." Cam looked up at me when I entered the room.

"Let me talk to your brother." I took a seat in front of Cam.

"Is there anything I can do to help you with this situation? You need to be focused on the game." I looked at him.

"Dad, I haven't thought about that game once, and I know that's a problem. This shit has me so fucked up, and Remi isn't willing to bend a little for me. That shit got me ready to explode on her ass. The only thing she did is agreed to let the kids stay the night here. When the wheels go up on that plane, I need her and my kids on it." He sighed, rubbing his hands down his face.

86

"Maybe she will let the kids come to the game with us, but in the midst of all of this, you still have a fiancée. If there is a problem with Saniya and your feelings for her, you need to let her know." I said what I needed to say and left him with his thoughts.

————

L ater that night, we were all sitting out on the patio drinking and smoking. Ever since we fucked around and ate some of Ma's weed cake, we've all been smoking, and she talks shit about us all the time. I love smoking that shit right before I slide inside of my wife. That shit is the best feeling in the world.

"You know ion know why Ma felt the need to get Trixie this lil' ugly nigga Harry for a boyfriend. Don't this nigga look funny as fuck in the face?" Gabe asked as he pulled on the blunt while Harry grilled his ass for talking shit about him. Trixie ass was staring at Gabe like he was a buttered down roll with some steak and potatoes. Harry ass hated Gabe, and every time he and Trixie was hanging out with Ma, Gabe tried to make Harry jealous.

"Keep fucking with Harry and he gone sucka slide yo' ass in the throat and put a hot one in yo' ass," Truth said to him, and we all fell out laughing.

"Tru, you need to stop smoking that shit 'cause you high as fuck if you think that lil' ugly muskrat lookin' nigga gone fuck with me. Don't ever get it fucked up, lil nigga. I will make you dig yo' own grave and climb in that bitch before I put the bullet in yo' dome. And don't make me take your girl, nigga." Gabe licked his tongue at Harry. Harry jumped up blowing all hard and shit. We were all high so that shit was extra funny.

"Nigga, I can't believe yo' ass is sitting here arguing and fuckin' with a damn monkey. Big Harry, fuck that nigga up the next time he comes for you!" Zelan laughed.

"Trix, you want some of this blunt with yo' sexy ass?" Gabe handed the blunt to Trixie, and she pulled on the shit so hard we all stopped talking to look at her ass.

"Yo, what's wrong with Trix?" Truth questioned, sitting up in his seat. We looked over at Trixie and her ass was just stuck. Just as we were about to get up to check on her, the ladies walked out onto the patio, and Trixie hit the ground. "Ohhhh shit! The fuck is going on!" Zelan yelled and we all jumped up.

"Trixie!" Ciera yelled, looking over at me franticly.

"Shit! Grams is fixing her a drink and was coming out to hang with us."

"I'm not getting a pulse; I think she's gone, y'all," Gia spoke, and I knew this was going to kill Ma.

"This song's dedicated to my homie and that gangsta leannn! Why you'd have to go so soon! I tip a 40 to your memmorryyyy!" Gabe started singing *Gangsta Lean by D.R.S.*

"Nigga, shut yo' dumb ass up, and you singing the shit wrong any damn way." Zelan shook his head.

"We have to do something y'all because Harry is about to lose his little monkey mind," Gia said, and Harry was holding Trixie in his arms, sounding like a broken record.

"Can we just bury her and try to go find a monkey just like her?" Gabe shrugged.

"Lawd, this nigga slow! Nigga, do you know how long Ma has had this damn monkey? She knows Trixie like the back of her hand. She will know that's not her damn monkey." Zelan was right. That was definitely not going to work.

"Chilllleeee, you betta watch J.R and Sue Ellen causeee

babbbby, they gone be hunchin' soon… Wha… What's wrong with my Trix! Trixxxiiieee, get up, baby!" She screamed.

"Ma, she was smoking the blunt and then passed out. There is no pulse, Ma. She's gone," Zelan told her, and she lost it.

"Ohhh lawd! Not my Trixie, lawd. You could've taken any one of these niggas, why you had to take my Trixie, lawd?" She cried out.

"Ion like that! Like how she gone tell the lawd he could have taken one of us? He did what he was 'spose to do. The good book says we don't know the day nor the hour. It was her time. I mean, I could see him taking that lil' ugly nigga right there, but he chose Trixie instead. God knows best. Maybe Trix was tiiieedd and needed her rest now." Gabe shrugged. Harry's ass must have been sick and tired of his ass because he jumped on Gabe so fast they hit the ground. This nigga was swinging and rolling on the ground fighting the fuckin' air. I swear I was damn near on my knees; this was not the time to be laughing. But this shit was too damn funny. We were all in a fit of laughter while Ma was holding onto Trixie.

"Harry, stop it and show some damn respect. My Trixie!" Ma yelled and Harry stopped fuckin' Gabe up.

"You lucky ion shoot yo' ass! Why y'all let that nigga jump on me like that? You know I get flashbacks and ion do creepy crawlers or ugly niggas. Jump yo'' ass over here again, and I bet you gone be one crispy ass nigga laying next to your girl," Gabe pulled the trigger on his torch gun. This dude had us bent the hell over in laughter.

"Juelz, can you make sure they get my baby off this ground? I wanna have a respectable funeral for my Trixie. Girls, I'm going to need y'all help making these arrangements. I need to go call my Santi and tell him he needs to come home." I felt bad for Ma.

89

She's had Trixie for a long time, so to see her like that was sad. Harry followed the ladies into the house. He was just as distraught as Ma was.

"Nigga, I can't believe you let a monkey beat yo' ass" Truth shook his head at Gabe.

"Tru, that nigga caught me off guard! I didn't want that nigga touching me," Gabe fussed.

"We need to pick her up and get her in the storage house." Zelan looked over at us.

"Nigga, where the hell you get this WE shit from? Ion want no monkey shit on me. Do they do like that final release of shit when they die?" This nigga was simple as hell, but I felt him on that shit. I called to have my staff come and take Trixie to the storage house until we could get her buried.

"Dad, Grams said Trixie is dead, and y'all killed her!" Kari said, running out onto the patio with Ju following behind her.

"Dang, Trix! Sorry to see you go, baby girl." Juju kneeled down to rub her hair.

"Ahhhh, hell nawl! How much time they give you for a monkey? Tru, you betta get us out of this shit. I done told you over and over again this family friendship shouldn't have lasted this damn long. These niggas are murderers first before anything else, all the way down to the fuckin' kids. Now, look. We might be going to jail on a murder one charge just cause Ma in her feelings over her dope fien ass monkey. This shit done killed my damn high. Somebody need to get Ma to roll another blunt for us." Gabe sighed, and we burst out laughing.

Even though we smoke weed, we damn sure didn't know how to roll a blunt. We always got Ma or Aunt Cynt to roll for us. After my staff came to move Trixie, we headed into the house to check on the ladies.

Chapter Thirteen

CAM

We were all sitting in the family room reminiscing about our time with Trixie and all the funny shit her and Grams got into.

"Ma, you remember when you were in charge of Lani and Mano's invitations to the wedding? My daddy almost shitted himself when Trix blasted that invitation on his ass." Uncle Gabe fell out laughing.

"Hunny, that shit was epic! My girl was always down for my foolishness." Grams laughed.

"I also remember Trix playing kissy-face with you while you were asleep, and yo' high ass thought it was Gia," Uncle Truth reminded Uncle Gabe, and we were all in here bent over. I loved the hell out of my family. When we got together, it was always a good time. Even shit with me and my dad was better. It was something about that interview that changed everything for us.

"Why you gotta bring up shit y'all promised to never bring up again? I was extra high and couldn't think for myself." He fanned us off because we were all damn near on the floor in laughter.

"That shit was so damn funny. When he realized he kissed Trix, his ass ran and jumped into the pool. Talkin' bout the chemicals would kill all the monkey contamination off his lips!" Aunt Ari said, which sent everybody into a fit of laughter again.

"Whatever!" Uncle Gabe's face was in a frown. He hated when they started on him, but loved making fun of everybody else. Remi was sitting at the bar with Laila, Kari, and her cousin Shan. Her mom had already gone upstairs with the kids. We invited them to stay the night with us because it was just too much media going on at Remi's place.

"Yooo, this family dope as shit. You need to make them chirren pappy yo' every day nigga, Rem!" Shan tried to whisper the shit, but that shit didn't work because I heard her and Kari's ass damn near choked on the drink she was sipping on.

"Shan!" Remi nudged her.

"Grams, do you need anything?" I asked her. I loved my grandmother, and I hated to see her hurting. They were in here acting up and messing with Grams, but Trixie was her companion, and she genuinely loved her.

"I'm going to be alright; it was just her time to go. All I know is me and my girl had one hell of a ride together." She wiped the tears from her eyes.

"Y'all sure did, Lai. You know Trix loved her some you," Aunt Cynt told her.

"Yeah, we sure did, Cynt." Grams smiled. She was always better when Aunt Cynt was around, and I'm glad she came rushing over for Grams.

"Ciera and Ari, I need y'all to get a venue and plan the services for Tuesday. Gia, your hair is always so sharp. Can you get your hairdresser to come here and do my Trixie hair for me? I will give them a bonus for coming up to do it," she said to Aunt Gia.

"I will call him now and see if he can swing it. He's a celebrity stylist, so he's always booked, but I'mma do my best, Ma."

"Kari, turn some music on and pour me and Lai a drink. We need to cheer her up." Aunt Cynt grabbed a blunt and lit it. I knew it was time for me to go. I don't need that shit in my system.

"You good, bro?" Ju asked, walking down the stairs.

"Yeah, I'm trying to get my head together," I told him.

"I got rid of some videos, but this is so high profiled the networks are even running with it. The moment I remove it, someone else has copied it already, and it's going back up."

"It's all good. It happened, and I lost my cool. If the nigga press charges, then that's what it is." I shrugged. We talked for a few more minutes before he went to join the family. I went into the kitchen to see what was up with Saniya. She's been walking around with an attitude toward me since I found out about my kids. Hell, I had to adjust to the news just like she did. Knowing I have kids changes everything for me now.

"I'll call you later." She ended the call and looked over at me.

"Who was that?" I asked her.

"My brother." Is all she said. Then she tried to walk past me, and I pulled her back to me.

"Listen, I'm not trying to make shit bad between us, Saniya. Ease up a little; those are my kids. Getting to know them and spending time with them is all I can think about right now. This is just as shocking to me as it is to you. All I'm asking is for you to support me while I work through this with

Remi and my children." I kissed her cheek, but she pushed away from me.

"First of all, you don't know if they're your kids, and I keep saying that shit to you. The bitch left school because she got pregnant. She didn't have money then and she damn sure doesn't have any now. And that's what this is about. She sees you out here doing good, and she needs something from you. I don't believe for one second that all of this shit was by accident. Nothing is going to come between us, and I mean that shit. I will never let some fake ass bitch come in and fuck up what we have!" She announced.

"Those are my kids; I don't need a DNA test to verify that shit for me. Niya, I had money when I met her back then, so her using me for money is bullshit, and you know it!" I was tired of hearing that shit from her.

"Fuck you, Cam!" She stormed out of the kitchen, and I decided to just sit here in my thoughts. Remi didn't want to come down to Atlanta so that I could be closer to the kids while I practiced for the game. She didn't want security following her. She refused the house my dad offered her earlier, and she wasn't sure if she would bring the kids to the game on Sunday. It's like she was ready to fight me at every turn, and that shit had me ready to tear some shit up. I needed to get my thoughts together and clear my mind because I needed my head in the game. It was going to be hard as fuck if I didn't get this straight with her about my son and daughter. A few minutes later, she came walking into the kitchen.

"I just wanted to say goodnight to you, and to let you know the kids are in the bedroom across the hall from mine with my mom." She just stood there playing with her hands like she did back in college. She always did that when she was nervous about something.

"Goodnight." I couldn't take my eyes off her, and it was as if she couldn't move. This girl was so fucking beautiful. I walked over and stood in front of her.

"Are you alright?" I asked, lifting her chin so that she could look at me. When she tried to move around me to leave the kitchen, I gripped her in my arms, crashing my lips onto hers. There was no fighting that shit. I knew this shit was wrong, but after kissing her last night, I couldn't stop thinking of all the ways I could use my tongue all over this fine ass body.

When she wrapped her arms around my neck, I lifted her into my arms as we deepened the kiss. Until she snatched away from me and ran out of the kitchen. I was playing with fire, and I knew it, but I wanted to be in her so fuckin' bad right now. I sat in the kitchen for about forty minutes trying to talk myself out of going up to her room and fucking the shit out of her.

Let's just say I lost the battle and was already in front of her bedroom door. This woman has been a secret addiction of mine since the day we slept together. I tried my best to forget her. I tried my hardest to stop thinking about her, but nothing worked. I tried finding another woman. It helped, but didn't stop her from creeping into my thoughts. I couldn't hold it. I have missed this woman and yearned for her for so fucking long.

I knocked on her door but didn't get an answer. When I turned the knob and eased inside, the sight before me had my damn knees about to buckle. Baby girl had this device in her hand going off on the pussy. "Fuck!"

She jumped.

"What are you doing?!" she stuttered. I locked the door and started removing every inch of my clothes. Nothing was going to stop me from invading her space and making love to the woman I'd been dreaming about every night since college. I took the vibrator from her hands and smiled down at her.

"Just one night, just give me one night with you, baby. I have been dreaming and thinking about you all these fuckin' years, Remi. I'm so fuckin' hungry for you!"

The moment her hands touched me; my body was on fire. I skillfully licked and sucked on her neck down to her breasts, sliding my fingers into her pussy and massaging her clit. The moment I placed the rose vibrator on her clit, her body lifted from the bed, and a moan escaped her lips. I worked this lil muthafucka on her clit so good, this damn girl was bustin' all over the place. Giving her a minute to calm down, I turned the sound bar on, and *Say What You Want by Usher x Zaytoven* came flowing through the speakers. Looking down at her beautiful naked body had my heart feeling like it was about to explode.

"Fuck, you wet!" I growled, sliding my fingers over her clit. I kissed, sucked, and licked from her breast to her thighs, gliding my tongue over her clit.

"I need you." She whimpered.

"Relax, baby and let me suck this cum out of you," I whispered, sucking her clit into my mouth. I was sucking and licking on that muthafucka like this was going to be my last time ever eating or fuckin' on some pussy. Spreading her legs further apart as I feasted on her pussy.

"Ohhhhh, Cam! Please don't stop. Shit!" She moaned out. Her body was shaking uncontrollably, and If I didn't know any better you would think this was the first time, she's ever had a man sucking on her pussy.

"Never, lil' mama," I gritted.

"My God, I'm cumming!" she screamed, and I quickly eased

into her, hearing her cry out the way she was did. Made me feel as if time stood fuckin' still, and history was repeating itself. I knew she wasn't a virgin because I took her virginity, and she gave birth to my kids. I tried to ease into her again, and she cried out as I pushed inside.

"Are you good? When was the last time you had sex, baby?" I asked her because she was so tight. She turned to look away, like she was embarrassed about something.

"How long?" I turned her to face me and looked down at her while stroking her nice and slow.

"Are you sure this is what you want because I got years to get off in this pussy tonight, and there isn't a soul that's gone stop me from doing that shit?" I pulled her bottom lip in between my teeth. The more I stroked her, the wetter she got, and the harder my dick got inside of her. My strokes became deeper and deeper. They were so powerful tears streamed down her face. It was like we were both fighting to stay right here in the moment, but that shit still wasn't enough. I knew I was wrong for doing this shit with my fiancée on the west wing of the house, but there was no way that I could stop.

"Fuck! This pussy so good!" I slammed into her repeatedly, pounding on her spot. I have never fucked a woman so hard, or had pussy feel so good in my life. I was losing it, and there was nothing I could do about it as cum began pouring out of me.

"Ohhh... Oh, fuck Cam! Fuck me! Ohhh God!" she screamed, closing her eyes.

"Open your fucking eyes and look at me when I'm inside of you!" I growled, giving her death strokes. "Fuck! Urggghhhh! Fuck!" I roared. Pulling out and flipping her over, I entered her so got damn deep it felt like I ruptured something. I had something to get off on her ass for keeping my kids from me! Oh yeah, this punishment dick is about to tear her life and pussy the fuck apart. The power in these strokes had her ass trying to run from the dick.

"Oh my God! Cam, please slow down." She pleaded. I pounded in her so fuckin' hard, I tried to break this muthafucka off in her.

"Stop fuckin' running and take this dick!" I gripped her ass, deep stroking her so damn deep, her ass couldn't do shit but moan.

"Mmmmmmm! Cameron, I'm so fucking sorry!" She screamed.

"Damn! I love fucking this wet ass pussy!" I was giving her these death strokes until she creamed all over this dick.

"Mmmmm, shit! Oh Godddd!" She cried out.

"Damn, I love this wet ass pussy…Fuckkkkk!" I gripped her ass, releasing inside of her. We just laid there in our thoughts for a few minutes, and then I eased out of her.

"What did we just do? Oh fuck! What did we dooo?! You're engaged, Cameron. We shouldn't have done that." She jumped out of bed, pacing back and forth. I got out of bed to calm her down.

"I'm sorry I put you in the situation, but I can't go back, Remi. Having you was a must for me, and now that I've had you, I won't make the same mistake again." I kissed her lips.

"Nooo, you have to go. This shouldn't have happened." She held her hands up to her face. I walked into the bathroom to clean up and put my clothes back on.

"We will talk about this later." I kissed her lips and left out of the room.

"Lawd, why am I always the vessel? Why am I always the one catching these lil' cheating ass Kassom kids, lawd? Don't ask me to hold yo' damn secret 'cause I ain't! Ion like the Lil' Slutville hoe you call yo' fiancée. Yessss, it's break-up season 'round this bitch! I'm in mourning, so ion feel bad 'bout shit, but my Trixie going on to glory!" Grams scared the shit out of me. I didn't even see her coming down the hall until she got up on me.

"Grams, it's not what it looks like." I was too damn embarrassed to look her in the face.

"Look at me, grandson. Oh, it looks like a lot to me." She snapped a picture of me with her phone and walked off.

"Grams!" I tried to whisper, hoping she would come back, but that shit didn't work and I damn sure didn't want to wake anybody up. Fuckkk!

"Wheewww chile. The shit show I'mma 'bout to start up in here is gone be one for the books!" she laughed, getting on the elevator.

"Grams, I know you're not a snitch," I called out to her. I knew she wouldn't do no shit like that, but with my Grams, you could never be too careful. Fuckkk!

Chapter Fourteen

REMI

I wanted so badly to get my mom, cousin, and kids and go home last night. Being around this man was going to cause me more pain than it would be happiness. He was engaged to be married, and yet I'm down on the other end of the hall fucking on this girl's man. I don't like her ass, but that still doesn't give me a reason to do what I did. That was a fucked-up decision that I would have to deal with.

That, in my eyes, was so fucked up, and I felt bad as hell about it. I can't stop thinking about the way he made love to me. It's been constantly on my mind, and my heart hurts for so many reasons. I grabbed my duffle bag and left the room because it was time for me to get my family and go home. Cam was due to go back to Atlanta, and I know he wanted me to just up and make provisions for the kids to be there with him. But I have a job, and I can't just up and leave at the drop of a dime. I still haven't heard from Zori, and now I'm worried. Stopping at the elevator, I grabbed my phone and dialed her number.

"Hey, girl. What's going on?" She asked.

"Seriously, Zori?! I've been calling you for the last two days. On top of that, I've been the headlines in The Shade room for two damn days!" I yelled. I really didn't mean to yell at her like that.

"You need to calm the hell down, Rem. I've been sick as hell for the past couple of days. I tried calling you to tell you I was sick, and to check on you because I got a message from Johnathan going off about you, Cam, and the kids. You might want to check your messages. Your phone kept going to voicemail. You know damn well I wouldn't just ignore you, Rem. I'm sorry that I put you in this predicament. If I didn't invite you to help with the interview, he probably wouldn't have found out about the kids." Zori sounded horrible, and I felt fucked up for not checking in on her.

"Zor, I'm so sorry. I'm just all over the place with everything. It's selfish of me to think that you're supposed too always be there for me."

"It's all good, sis. You know I love you, girl. I'm about to get up and try to take a shower. Let me call you back in a few minutes."

"Ok. Let me know if you need anything and I will bring it over for you, friend." We ended the call, and I got on the elevator. My mom and Shan were already downstairs having breakfast with the kids and the Kassom family. When I walked into the kitchen, all eyes were on me.

"Hey, cuz. How did you sleep?" Shan asked with a damn smirk on her face.

"Good morning. I slept fine."

"You got that good, good wood... Oh. I mean, that's good." She smiled, and Cam spit out the drink he was drinking.

"Are you alright, baby?" Saniya asked, patting him on his back.

"Remi, please get you some breakfast," Ms. Ciera offered.

"Mommy, we got pancakes, and Papa is going to take me on a plane ride to buy me a doll baby! Right, papa?" Kammy had the biggest smile spread across her face, looking over at Juelz.

"That's right, baby." He smiled, looking over at Ciera for help.

"Kaleb, I heard you can name all the presidents and the year they were elected?" JuJu asked Kaleb.

"Yep, that's old, though. I knew that when I was four. I know where they were born, who their parents are, their birth dates, their spouses' names and birthdates, their children, and their birth dates. The list goes on and on," Kaleb revealed, stuffing his little mouth with pancakes.

"Damn Ju, my lil' great nephew is educational smart. He's not a young criminal-minded kid like your ass was," Zelan teased JuJu.

"Yeah, at least his ass ain't selling shit on the black market and breaking in your daddy bank online passing out money like that shit was free food stamps just because he wanted to help folk for Christmas." Gabe shook his head.

"I know how to do codes and break through firewalls too. That's fun to do, but my mommy said that's bad, and I can't do it." He shrugged his little shoulders, crunching on a piece of bacon. Cam damn near coughed up a lung from choking on his food.

"Oh shit!" Ari blurted. We all turned in the direction she was looking in, and it was just Ms. Lai. I turned back to fix my plate, but it was something about Ms. Lai. I turned back to look at her. She had on a t-shirt that said '**Slutville, yo' nigga cheatin'**

cheatin'!' The picture on the shirt was blurry, but I swear it looked like Cam. And it had an arrow under the picture.

"Morrrnnning! What's for breakfast because I woke up hungry as hell this morning? Chile, them hallways was talking summin' serious last night! Somebody was getting it theee hell in, hunny!" I looked around the room, embarrassed, wondering if she was talking about me and Cam.

"That was that 'I want that ole thing back' talk last night," Shan blurted.

"Damn sure was!" Ms. Lai ran over and high-fived her. I moved to the other side of the breakfast bar to finish fixing my plate.

"Remi, you alright? I see you got a lil' limp. It was that hook that got you, huh!" Ms. Lai fell out laughing.

"Grams!" Ciera yelled.

"Ciera, shut the hell up! I'm trying to save you from having the daughter-in-law from hell," she told her.

"Ma, what the hell you got on? Who the fuck cheatin'?" Zelan asked her. She started moving her eyes wide in the direction of Cam and then stood by me at the bar with the damn arrow on her shirt pointing at me.

"You know what? I'm sick of this disrespectful shit! Cameron, let's go!" Saniya jumped up.

"Watch your mouth in front of my kids, nieces, and nephews," Cam gritted.

"Fuck that! I'm sick of hearing these your kids. You don't know these kids, and we're just supposed to let they ass into our world. All because this bitch said you're the daddy and because they favor your mom! Since I've been..." I cut that bitch off, punching the shit out of her. Beating this bitch's ass was the only thing on my mind right now. I wanted blood, and I wasn't stopping until I got that shit! The shit with me and this hoe was long overdue. I felt someone pulling me off her, and I was still trying to get to her ass.

"Bitch, just because you got his so-called kids, you think that's gone do something? That's my man, and your ass is just jealous because he's about to marry me and have babies with me! You wasn't the bitch he wanted in school, and you're damn sure not what he wants now! Stupid bitch!" Saniya screamed while Cam held onto her.

"I can't tell! The way he caressed my insides last night, let's me know I was everything he wanted! Ohh, and another thing. I know Cam's the father of my kids because he's the only man I've ever been with! Stupid bitch! Where are my fucking kids?!" I yelled, and the look on his face let me know he wasn't expecting me to say that.

"Ohhh shit!" I heard someone yell out.

"Hell to the nawl! I couldn't wait on no nigga that long. Mmmm, mmmm! Wheeeww, you deserved every cheating inch you got last night, hunny! Cause ain't that much *I'mma wait on my nigga* in the world!" Ms. Lai shook her head in disbelief.

Just as I was about to turn to leave, Saniya broke free, running up on me, swinging. I cracked that hoe dead in her shit, and this time I got blood outta her ass. I was mad as fuck, and Cam looked defeated. Fuck him too right now. We were going blow for blow up in this kitchen, and I damn sure wanted to tear this bitch up in here. I know I was wrong for that, but I don't give a fuck about hurting her feelings. She should have kept my kids out of it. I acted out of character. I've been mixed up in more bullshit in three days with Cam and his bitch than I have ever been in. The tears streamed down my face as I was being pulled off her again.

"Yessssssuhh! It wouldn't be a Kassom family gathering without a kitchen brawl! And I got bets that this shit ain't over," Uncle Gabe said, pulling money out and sitting it on the table. I didn't see my mom or kids, and I'm glad she got them out of here.

"Shan, let's go." I walked out of the kitchen without looking back at any of them. My mom and Ciera was in the family room with the kids. I grabbed Kaleb and Kamryn and headed for the door. We kept moving, even though I could hear screaming and yelling in the kitchen. I didn't drive my car, so we got in the truck that they assigned to us.

"Remi!" Cam came out of the house with his fist balled up. I hate shit happened this way, but fuck it, I said what I said. He walked past me and went straight to the kids.

"Daddy has to go back home for my upcoming game. If your mom doesn't bring you down to see me soon, I promise you both I will be back to see you. Here is a phone. Anytime you want to facetime me, you can." Cam hugged and kissed his kids, helping them get into the car.

"I'll be in touch." Is all he said and walked off.

"Cuz, you blew up the spot big time on they ass. Damn!"

Chapter Fifteen

CAM

I wasn't expecting shit to pop off like that, and I damn sure wasn't expecting Remi to let everyone know that we were together last night. She put it out there, and I wasn't going to sit and lie about it.

"I can't believe you, nigga! So that's how playing it? You just think you gone fuck that bitch and it's supposed to be all good with us!" Saniya yelled. There was no way that I was going to lie about it. Things with me and Saniya haven't been the best for a long time. We haven't seen eye to eye on shit and she hated my family. To be honest, I'm not sure why I've stayed with her for as long as I have. We've been on and off for years, and I think it's just time for us to go our separate ways. When I saw Remi, everything I felt for her just came rushing back, and being with her last night only made matters worse.

"Saniya, I'm sorry for hurting you, and I feel fucked up about it. I'm all over the place, and I know I'm just meeting my children, but the issues you have with them, and their mother isn't good. Your mouth is reckless, and they're listening to you talk shit about them. That shit is not cool. Remi is grown and can handle herself, but my kids are all me. Look, sleeping with Remi wasn't planned. It just happened, but it opened my eyes to say that I'm not ready to get married. You don't deserve a nigga to half love you. I'm not going to sit here and give you half of me when my heart belongs to someone else.

This shit is hard to say, but it needs to be said, and I hate that it's all coming out here and now. I hate that it wasn't until I saw Remi that realization kicked in. You may think this is all Remi's fault. Or none of this would have happened if we didn't run into Remi. Truth be told, I probably wouldn't have gone through with it. Niya, I love you. I just don't love you enough to marry you." I looked at her. This was the realest shit I've ever spit.

"You think I'mma let shit go just like that? Nigga, you ain't going no muthafuckin' where. That bitch may have fucked you last night, but that's the only fuck she gone get from you. We're still getting married. As a matter of fact, I think we should move our date up. I'm in the marrying mood this month. You think I did all this work to get and keep your ass, just to hand you over to the bitch that I did everything to get rid of? Yeah, ok!" She chuckled, and I'm sitting here trying to figure out what the fuck she meant by doing everything to get rid of Remi.

"The fuck are you talking about?! You don't have a choice in the matter. You can't make me be with you if that's not really what I want, and why would you want to force some shit like that? You know shit has been on the edge with us even before Remi came back into the picture. So, stop acting like shit was good a week ago when it wasn't." I didn't want to do this shit with her. This shit was about to get out of hand. I could feel it.

"No, nigga! You don't have a choice about this shit. Don't ever try to fuck with a bitch like me! I can be your worst fuckin' nightmare!" She threw her phone on the bed and I picked it up. It was a video playing of me and this dude Zeno back in my freshmen year. We were out one night, and he asked me to help him with this drop, and I did it. So, I guess the nigga recorded me doing the pickup, and the video shows me holding the bag of cocaine in my hand.

"The fuck! Where did you get this shit from?" I asked her. I could feel the temperature in my body rising because I know this bitch not doing what the fuck I think she's doing.

"If something happens to me, and or if my people can't get in touch with me, this video goes to the NFL, the police, and the media. I will fuckin' finish you and this family! Oh, and that prenup bullshit is a no for me. Everything they out here saying about me is true! I want all the fuckin' money. I knew you would be my ticket to richness. You can tell that bitch Remi you don't want her or them kids. I see she still made something of herself, even after I reported her and Johnathan for cheating." She laughed.

"Bitch! You think this shit a game? You coming for me threatening my fuckin' freedom, and career?!" I gripped her ass up with my hand wrapped around her fuckin' throat. I didn't want to go to jail on a murder charge, so I dropped the hoe to the floor. I can't believe this shit! My freshman year in school, I was reckless. I was doing so much shit, I almost got kicked out. Then me and my dad were going through it so much, he cut me off financially. I knew I could get money from my mom, brother, sister, or my grandmother, but I wanted him to know I didn't need him.

Now, look at how the fucked-up decisions I made back then are coming back to haunt me now. I'm gone play her game, but she better know my get back is gone be unstoppable. This bitch fuckin' don't know who she's fucking with! I'm a muthafuckin' Kassom and I bust my guns like one!

Chapter Sixteen

KARI

Trixie's Funeral

Today was the day that we lay Trixie to rest. Cam couldn't be here because he was practicing for his game on Sunday. The flowers he sent Grams this morning made her smile. Something seemed off with my brother, and I can't wait to get back home to Atlanta to make sure he's really good. I know him and Saniya were going through some things ever since Remi gave her the business. She didn't tell us nothing we didn't already know. Grams sent out a group text to me, Ju, Laila, Aunt Ari, and Remi's cousin Shan last night, along with a picture of Cam leaving Remi's room. We got a whole damn text thread of gossiping about they ass going on. That damn Shan fit right on in with the foolishness we had going on. We were all team Remi and prayed Cam saw through Saniya's bullshit. Grams said the next time we're all together, she wanted Myia to drop something in her food to wipe her ass out in a matter of seconds. Grams wanted that bitch dead-dead if she wanted the Diamond clique on her ass.

"Gia, what time is your friend coming to do Trix's hair?" Grams questioned Aunt Gia when she walked into the family room.

"He's at the gate going through security now, Grams." Grams was right to put Aunt Gia in charge of the hair because dude be hooking her ass up. My aunt's hair is always on point.

"Ma, you really gone let Gabe and Tay preach this monkey funeral? I can't even believe we sitting here entertaining you with this funeral. You could have been buried Trix ass." Uncle Zelan walked up to the bar to pour him a drink.

"Yes, and you need to start getting ready 'cause as soon as they do Trixie's hair, the funeral is going to start," she cried.

"You got to be strong, hermosa (beautiful)," Pop Santiago said, wiping the tears from her eyes. My mom and dad had this company come out and setup an outdoor tent with a floor for Trixie's services.

"They have it set up so nice out there for our girl, Lai. It's so many beautiful flowers. I know Trix smiling down on us after seeing how the family is coming together." Aunt Cynt told Grams walking into the family room.

"Ma! Do Juelz know you got that dead ass ape in the house laying on his two thousand dollar sheets?" Uncle Gabe asked, and I was holding my head.

"I thought the damn monkey was in the storage room out back?" Uncle Z looked at Grams.

"I couldn't just leave my Trixie out there like that. Y'all know she's scared of the dark." Grams shrugged.

"She dead! It's gone be dark for fuckin' ever!" Uncle Gabe shouted. "And this lil' tent setup better have some damn heat in it 'cause I can't preach under cold conditions," he fussed, and we all laughed, agreeing with him. But knowing my bougie ass mom, that tent is hooked up.

"It's not that cold out, but you will think you were in a building. It's very warm and nice out there. Ciera, Ari, and Juelz really did a great job putting this together," Aunt Cynt explained as she lit a blunt.

"Let me hit that blunt so it can help me see this good book better when I'm up there giving the word." Uncle Gabe had us in here cracking the hell up.

"Ma, this is my stylist, Darius," Aunt Gia introduced her stylist to everyone.

"It's nice to meet everybody. Ms. Laila, I'm going to make your daughter's hair so beautiful. I'm so sorry for your loss," he said to Grams. I wonder if Aunt Gia told her stylist that Trixie was an actual monkey. He was gay, so I know this shit was going to be extra funny. Me and Laila decided to go with them to the room she had Trixie in. Aunt Gia opened the door, and we all walked into the room. Grams had the canopy curtains around the bed, so we had to pull them back. Darius jumped back, damn near knocking me over.

"Gia, girl, what the fuck is that?! Hell to the nawl, Bihhhh! What in the rich people monkey shit is this?! This that shit ion fuck with. Like who has a rich dead monkey trying to get they damn hair done? Aht to the fuck Aht, bitch. Y'all better blow dry that shit out and throw some pink bows in it 'cause babbbbby, not the fuck I. Fuck all that and that damn money she trying to give me. I'm not putting none of my good shit in that thang hair. That nigga might got monkey lice.

Wheeewwww, this ain't givin' what it's 'sposeee to give, hunny. I'm supposed to be wrapped up with my man in

Atlantic City this weekend, and you got me over here fuckin' with a dead monkey. The devil is a liar, and you a hoe for this hoe shit right here! I hope yo' pussy freeze the fuck up, and you get a Charlie horse when you 'bout to bust the best nut of your entire fuckin' life. May yo' titties dry up, and yo' pussy turn to dust for this hoe ass shit!" Darius fussed while me, Laila, Aunt Toya, and Aunt Gia were hanging on for dear life. My got damn side was in severe pain. I knew this dude was going to act the fuck up.

"Is everything alright in here?" Dad asked, walking into the room.

"Good lawd! Father, I know you know my heart, and I know you wouldn't just place this beautiful nigga in my presence if it wasn't a sign from you, gawd! I will be obedient in yo' name cause lawd, this nigga is extra extraordinary. They don't make fine like this no more," he mumbled under his breath, fanning himself. When Uncle Truth, Uncle Meek, and Uncle Zelan walked in, he damn near fainted.

"Who is this nigga?" Uncle Zelan looked at us.

"This is my friend Darius, and he's here to do Trixie's hair." Aunt Gia smiled.

"Why does Ma have her dead ass in my house in the bed?!" My dad was pissed. The guys left the room, and we finally talked Darius into helping with Trixie's hair. About an hour later, Trixie's hair was done, and she was dressed in a white gown like her ass was going to prom, with some red bottoms on. Grams had Trix dressed to the gawds that's for sure. I wanted to laugh so damn hard because this dude gave her some weave and did a fly ass feathered bob.

"Damn, you got Trix fly as fuck. I might have to let you hook me up if you're ever in the A," Laila said to Darius.

"My best friend lives there. I'm always in Atlanta." He looked over at her.

"That's cool. I think we better get dressed; it's almost time for the service," Laila stated.

"Y'all really about to have a funeral for this damn monkey?" He looked at us like we were crazy.

"Real life, my grams don't play about her Trixie. You should stick around and party with us afterward," I invited him, and he agreed.

"Gia, show me to the alcohol 'cause I need me a drink or two or three." He shook his head. We all went our separate ways to get dressed.

"Babe, you look beautiful. Let's go before Grams kicks our ass for being late." Jah kissed my lips. Once I was done getting dressed, we went downstairs, and Aunt Tay and Uncle Gabe asses were smoking and damn drinking.

"Bruh, take this blunt while I fill my flask up." Aunt Tay passed the blunt and went over to the bar.

"We gotta stop getting high, 'cause my ass ain't gone be able to read nothing in the good book other than telling them damn people it was a good book." Uncle Gabe laughed, taking another shot.

"Shit, I feel you. We gone just talk about dumb shit, say a few words of the word and let these people eat up all this free food."

"Are y'all ready?" Aunt Ari walked into the room with Uncle Z behind her.

"I know damn well y'all niggas not high. Tay, your damn eyes look like they about to close. How many fingers I'm holding up?" Uncle Z asked her.

"Three fingers and a thumb! I'm good; we got this." She was stretching her eyes wide as hell, and that shit was so funny. We all walked outside into the tent, and I swear this shit was insane. Grams was at it again. She had shit setup like she did at Mano & Melani's wedding. She had monkeys every damn where, strapped and ready for war.

"Ion mean to be rude, but is it too late for me to leave? I just remembered my mama needed something from the store," Darius said, taking his seat next to me and Aunt Gia. For the life of me, I don't know where she gets the fascination with monkeys from. Harry was sitting up front, staring at Trix like he wanted to get in the casket with her. We took our seats as the choir sang, *I Give Myself Away by William McDowell. Yes*, Grams had a damn choir!

"All these damn monkeys is making me uncomfortable, but I need to record this shit 'cause ain't nobody gone believe this shit at all." Darius pulled his phone out and started recording.

"How she get a choir, and she an old school sinner?" Uncle Zelan asked as we took our seats. Grams, Pop Santi, Aunt Cynt, Johan, my dad, and mom all walked in, and Grams was a mess as the choir continued to sing.

"Trixxxxxiieee! Come bacckkkk, Trix!!!" Grams screamed as they walked up to the casket.

"Wheew lawd, is all that hollering necessary?" Darius whispered to Aunt Gia.

"Praiseee the lawd, saints! We here today 'cause po' lil' Trixie gone to monkey heaven. One thing I can say about Trixie, she lived her life the way she wanted to live it. She didn't care that I had a wife; she loved me anyway! We loved her, but God loved her best. He needed His child with Him! There gone be a day and time that your name gone be called to go on home to glory! This ain't the time to be sad. You need to stand on your feet and give Gawd the highest praise and celebrate Trixie's life!" Uncle

Gabe shouted, and we were on our damn feet clapping and shit all into it.

"You know Gawd gone always show up and show out every time, praise God! Mmmmmshakkalakalaka!" Aunt Tay yelled out and dropped the mic.

"Whet in the Pentecostal, Seventh-day Adventist, Baptist church is going on in here?!" Darius stated, and he had me, Laila, Aunt Toya and Aunt Gia bent over. I could hang with this dude any day of the week because he had my ass in tears. He was looking around, amazed that we went all out and had on our good shit for Trix.

"The doors of the church are opened. Choir, give us a selection while the family comes and say their goodbyes to our beloved." Uncle Gabe held his hands out.

"Does he know that this not a real church? This a tent?" Darius was a damn fool. The choir started singing *Going Up To Yonda*. They tried to get Grams to go up there, but she was too distraught, and Harry was stretched out on the floor crying his monkey tears. Uncle Gabe, Uncle Zelan, Uncle Meek, and my dad walked up to the casket to say their goodbyes. When Uncle Gabe touched Trixie's arm, this heifer jumped up, standing in the casket, and pointing the AK Grams had put in her casket. Her monkey friends done pulled their guns too. That caused my dad and uncles to pull theirs. Darius' ass slid out of the chair onto the floor, holding onto Aunt Gia's leg.

"Lawd, this ain't it. I know you didn't bring me this far to leave me! I come to you as a scared hoe in my time of need. I just got my new house, and business is booming. Please Lawd, don't let monkey nation take me out. I know in your house there are many mansions, but I wanna live in my mini mansion in Cove Manor subdivision in New Jersey lawd. I probably want be ready to see your mansions until I'm a hundred. Stop giving these rich people so much money, lawd. They start doing dumb shit wit' it, Lawd.

I'm not ready to die, Father! *One of these mornings won't be very longggg.* Lawd, ion wanna walk around heaven all day right now. I'mma listen to you about me attracting these bad body bitches in my life. Gia bad body ass knew what she was doing, and now she done got me caught theee hell up over ten thousand dollars. If you spare me, Lawd, I swear I'mma quit all that shit with Jeremy and be faithful to Rick and Shawn. In yo' name, Lawd!" Darius prayed, and we were in real tears.

"Trixie girl! You're alive! Girl, you can't be hittin' the blunts so hard like that. The shit knocked you out for almost three damn days, Trix! Gawd gave you back to me, so we can't smoke on Sundays no mo'." Grams helped Trixie out of the casket and they walked out of the tent.

"So, this lil nigga hit the ground 'cause she hit the blunt too hard and her high ass been in a deep ass sleep?! Man, I'm going to get high and go home to fuck on my wife for the rest of the day!" Uncle Zelan shook his head. This has been one crazy ass day, but I have definitely got enough laughs to last me a lifetime.

Chapter Seventeen
⟋⟍

SANIYA

Cam thinks this shit was a game, but I'm not playing with his ass. He was going to do what I wanted when the fuck I wanted it. I hate that it had to come to this, but this nigga wasn't about to leave me for this bitch now. I went through too much shit to keep her away to just lose everything in four fuckin' days.

"You need to stop all that damn pacing back and forth. I told you this shit was going to backfire on your ass. You should have left that girl alone back in school. You knew him coming here to do that interview was a bad move, and you were supposed to stop him from doing it in the first place. It's not like you didn't know she worked for the fucking network!" Zori threw her hands in the air. I was back in New York trying to figure out my next move regarding this bitch Remi and her kids.

"If you just did what the fuck you were supposed to do none of this shit would've happened. How the fuck did she end up at the house?! If she didn't come, he wouldn't have ever thought about her ass again! And just like that, this bitch fucks him, and now he wants out of the relationship. Thank GOD we had that video of him with the drugs back in school. I knew that shit would come in handy one day. Now we gone be rich as fuck because of it. Cam knows the deal. If he wants to remain a free man, he gone marry me, and we gone keep living off of his fuckin money!" I'm going to get everything I want, and that includes his fine ass. I love everything about that man, down to his dirty fuckin' drawls.

"We could have been used that video and just took the nigga for his money a long time ago. It's more to it than what you're letting on. You love that man, and the fact that you sitting here playing in my face is pissing me off. I've been playing your fool for six fuckin' years, and you never had any intentions of leaving him. Now you out here threatening him if he don't marry you?! Make that shit make sense 'cause right now I smell bullshit!" Zori yelled.

"So, you don't trust that I got us? I've always made sure that you were straight. Me marrying him only makes shit better for the both of us," I tried to explain to her. Of course, I have to fill Zori's head with bullshit. I've had her fine ass wrapped around my finger for years. As long as I took care of her, and made her feel like it was gone be us in the end, she would do whatever the fuck I wanted her to do. She's the one that talked Remi into going back home to have her baby and quitting school.

I knew she was pregnant with Cam's baby the day she found out. I was feeding Zori all the bullshit to tell her. Keeping this bitch away from him for all these years took a lot of time, money, and energy. Ain't no way I'mma let this bitch just come take my man. My financial freedom was more important than some nerdy ass bitch and her kids. Besides, the dick between that nigga's thighs had my ass mentally gone! He was right. Our relationship has been rocky, but I kept playing my part. Cam hates to see any woman cry, and just when I thought I was losing him, I just started my waterworks, threw this pussy on him, and we were good again.

The thing that we fought about the most was his family. I couldn't stand none of them bitches, and if there was ever an opportunity, his mama, grandma, and sister would definitely get a bullet. Every time he went home to see them, I did my best not to go with him. The only reason I went this time was because of that interview. Yeah, I knew everything about Remi because Zori kept me updated on everything and played her muthafuckin' part. She played the fuck out of being the supportive friend to Remi all these years. She said she didn't know Remi was going to be at the interview, but something tells me she knows more than she's letting on. All I know is she better not fuck up, 'cause this shit gone get ugly.

Chapter Eighteen

REMI

Cam and I haven't really spoken since the incident at his parent's house last weekend. I've only spoken to him through Kaleb and Kamryn. Of course, they speak to him every night before they go to bed. The kids were so excited about their dad's game, and when he asked if they could come, I couldn't say no. Cam offered for us to fly with his family, but I declined because I guess I was still a little embarrassed about what I did. We arrived in Atlanta a few hours ago, and finally got settled into our hotel. The kids had just finished eating dinner and taking their baths for bed. Cam had practice and said he would be here after he was finished. About thirty minutes later, I heard a knock at the door, and I peeped through the peephole and saw that it was Cam.

"Hey." I smiled, stepping out of the way.

"Hey, sorry I'm late. Are they asleep already?" He walked inside, closing the door behind him.

"Yeah, they had a really long day. You can go say goodnight.

121

I'm sure someone will pop up at the sound of your voice." They had just fallen asleep, but I knew Kamryn would wake up if she heard her dad's voice. That little girl was so in love with her father, and it's gotten worse since she met him in person. Cam headed to the back, where the bedrooms were in the penthouse suite that he booked for us. I decided to let him say goodnight to them in private.

Grabbing my ringing phone, it was Shan calling me. Her and my mom went back to South Carolina a few days ago. I ignored her call and told her that Cam was here to visit the kids and I would call her when he left. A few minutes later, he walked back out into the living room area, walked over to the bar, and poured a drink.

"Were they sleeping?" I asked. He was sipping on his drink and staring at me so damn hard it made me feel uncomfortable. I owed him an apology for what I did, and this was the best time to give it to him.

"Cam, I know we haven't talked much since the incident at your parents' house. I'm really sorry about what I did, and I pray that I didn't mess anything up with you and Saniya. It wasn't my intention to come in between what y'all have going on." I looked over at him, but he just sipped his drink, still watching me.

"Cam," I called out.

"You're sorry, huh?! Does your pussy feel the same way, or is it just your conscience that's sorry, baby? Because I'm not sorry about a muthafuckin' thing. The only thing I'm sorry about is not being able to fuck you when I want you."

"I don't think we should do that again. You're with her, and it's clear that's where you want to be." I didn't want to complicate things, and I damn sure didn't want things to be awkward with us every time we saw each other.

"Is it true, Rem?"

"Excuse me? Is what true?" I asked in confusion.

"That you love me enough to save yourself for me? Because I love the shit out of you, baby. I've always loved you. I fought my hardest not to love you because I thought you chose that nigga. It's been six years, and I'm the only man you've been with? You love me that much, lil mama? That shit has been on my mind since the day you said it." He walked over to me, invading my personal space. My body started to tremble, hearing him say he loved me. I was so damn nervous having him so close to me, so I dropped my head to avoid his stare. He lifted my chin, staring me deep in my eyes. The way he looked at me wouldn't let me look away.

"I guess it really doesn't matter anymore. You're about to be a married man soon. The only thing we have between us are those two beautiful babies down the hall." I pointed in the direction of the bedrooms.

He chuckled, stepping away and walking back over to the bar. "You're right. If that's how you feel, that's how you feel. I can't make you say some shit you don't mean. My bad, lil mama." He downed his drink and stood to leave. He stopped when I jumped up, waiting for me to say something. I was having a battle with myself because I was so confused. I loved this man. I have never in my life loved any human more than I loved this guy until I had my kids. I guess my silence caused him to move towards the door again.

"Yes, I've loved you from the moment you opened the door for your first tutoring lesson. I knew you wouldn't be interested in someone like me, and the moment you entered me, I vowed to never love another or give myself to another man. When I found out I was pregnant with your children, that promise was sealed. I only wanted to have your babies, Cameron. Hell, I'm still in love with you. Every day, I dream about you. I've been dreaming about you for over six fucking years. I only wanted to remember and feel the way you caressed my walls. My heart and love was designed for you." I poured all out on the table for him as the tears streamed down my face.

"Damn!" he murmured.

"I love you so much, Cameron, and I've been waiting to tell you that. I didn't tell you about them, and I'm so sorry for making such a grave mistake. You didn't deserve that, and I regret every decision I ever made about that situation. I'm so, so, so fucking sorry. I've missed you so much, and now our lives are different. I dreamed so many days that you would find us, forgive me, and become my husband. Shit just don't always work out the way you dream it or plan it." I shrugged, crying so damn hard my chest was heaving in and out. I felt like I was having a heart attack. My chest hurt so much. I was a complete mess. Everything that I had been holding in all of those years was being poured out in this room tonight. This wasn't the type of meeting that I thought we would be having. Every emotion and every truth we've had between us came out, and it was fuckin' needed. The love for this man was so real, and I needed him to feel it and believe it.

He lifted me into his arms, pinning me against the door, and our tongues hungrily attacked one another. The way this man aggressively sucked and licked my neck had me on fire for him. I could barely catch my breath. My need for him was so severe I was involuntarily cumming.

We were both trying to get out of our clothes while he still had me pent against the door. All I know is I wanted this man so deep inside of me, and if he ripped some shit in the process, he would have to take me to get checked out afterward. The moment he slid the head of his dick up and down my slit, had me crying out for him.

"Cameron, please give it to me." He wasted no time entering me with force. I cried out like a wounded animal as he moved in and out of me with deep, slow strokes.

"You know how much I love you, baby. I promise you I'm going to fix this shit. You have to promise me you will wait for me, Rem." He picked up his pace, slamming into me over and over again. I was holding on for dear life as I dug my nails into his back.

"Promise...Fuck! Promise me you will wait for me, baby!" It damn near sounded like he was pleading with me. I looked into his eyes, and that's how we both connected. I met his thrust, grinding up and down on his dick as we gazed deeply into each other's eyes. That night, our love for one another won this battle. I reconnected with the man that I've loved for years, and there was no way I could let go of him. Saniya was his fiancée, and I know I might be wrong for thinking this way, but I'm willing to fight to change his mind. His kids and I need him, and I pray our love is strong enough. For hours, this man had me cumming and crying so much, I almost forgot our kids were in this suite with us. I'm so glad we didn't wake them up. I felt a pain in my heart when Cam crawled out of my bed to go home to his fiancé.

Chapter Nineteen

CAM

It was game day, and I just couldn't pull myself out of this bullshit ass mindset I was in. This shit with Saniya was fuckin' with me heavy. I can't believe I fucked up the way I did with her. I hated this bitch and wanted her the fuck away from me, but I didn't want to take no chances with her. I knew if I went to my dad, he would blow his fuckin' top over this shit. I didn't know how the fuck I was gonna get out of this shit because I damn sure didn't want her to bring my family down behind something I did.

"Good morning, husband to-be." She tried to kiss me, and I swerved her ass.

"Don't put your fuckin' hands on me." This bitch had me ready to put a bullet in her ass, no cap.

"Ahhhhh, so now you mad? You're the one out here fucking around on me, and now you mad because I came for some getback! Oh, it's gone be a lot of getback, and since you gave that bitch some kids, I want a baby, and we're going to start tonight when you win this playoff game." She smiled, rubbing her stomach.

"Let me tell you something. You will never be Remi, bitch!" I nudged her ass, walking out. Jumping in my car, I sped out of the driveway. It was a little too early to be heading to the stadium, and I didn't want to go to my parents' house. Since three of their kids lived in Atlanta, they bought a house here. I decided to stop by Kari's before I headed over to the hotel to see Remi and the kids. I put the security code in the keypad and waited for the gates to open. I know as soon as Saniya sees Remi and the kids at the game, she's going to lose her damn mind. Kammy has been asking me all week about the game, and I didn't want to disappoint her and Kaleb. I wanted them to be here for it, and that's what the fuck it is. I rang the doorbell and waited for someone to come to the door.

"Sup, bro?" Jah dapped me up, and I walked inside.

"What's going on with y'all?" I asked Jah, just as my niece Pai came running down the stairs and into my arms for a hug.

"Uncle Cam, don't forget you're supposed to take me shopping." She reminded me.

"I got you, baby girl." I smiled, walking into the kitchen to see Kari, Ju, and Myia talking.

"Sup?" I kissed Kari and Myia on the cheek and dapped Ju up.

"You ready for the big game, bro?" Ju asked.

"Yeah, I'm as ready as I'm gonna get." I sighed, taking a seat at the table.

"What's wrong? You should be pumped up and excited about today." Kari was right, but I was stressed the fuck out. I wanted to tell them what was going on with me, but they had to keep this shit between us. Maybe if we all put our heads together, we can figure out how to get me out of this shit.

"I got something I need to talk to you guys about. Saniya is blackmailing me-" I was cut off by the doorbell going off. Jah went to grab the door, while Kari and Ju were looking over at me.

"What the fuck do you mean she's blackmailing you?" Kari was on her feet. I wanted to wait to see who it was at the door because I didn't want dad to know right now.

"That's probably Remi. I spoke to her earlier and invited her, and the kids to come ride with us to the game. Dad rented four party buses for all of us to get to the stadium. Now tell us what the hell you're talking about!"

"Daddy!" Kaleb and Kammy ran over to me, and I lifted them both into my arms.

"Hey, look at you two with Daddy's jersey on." Seeing them and their mom with my Jersey on definitely lifted my spirits.

"Bro, tell us what's going on." Ju sat up in his seat. I looked over at Remi and I knew I could trust her.

"I tried to break it off with Saniya after Remi said that we were together at mom and dad's. She showed me a video of me doing a pickup from someone and then pulling the cocaine out of the bag. I don't know who recorded me, but this happened back in my freshmen year when I was out there running wild. It was around the time that dad cut me off." I shrugged, disappointed in myself.

"Oh my god! This shit could ruin you if it gets out." Kari jumped up, pacing back and forth, and my brother left the room.

"Are you alright? I'm so sorry." Remi placed her hand in mine.

"I'm fucked up over this shit. She wants to move our wedding up, and she wants me to marry her without a prenup." I shook my head.

"Oh, really?! This bitch is crazy as fuck if she thinks we about to let her play with us. We not the muthafuckin' family to be threatening. Baby bro, you go ahead and play your heart out today. We got this lightweight shit. The less y'all know, the better," Kari explained as Myia got on her phone and walked out of the kitchen.

"Cam, how did she show you the video?" Ju questioned, walking back into the kitchen with his laptop.

"Auntie Kari, can I have your Wi-Fi ID and password, please?" Kaleb ran into the kitchen with his iPad.

"Kaleb, give us a minute, baby," Remi told him, but Kari gave him the information to sign into the internet.

"She showed me on her phone, Ju." He started working on his laptop for a few minutes, and five minutes later, he had Saniya's cell phone mirrored on his laptop. We went through her phone, and she had a lot of videos of us fuckin', and that shit was weird because I didn't know she was recording us with that shit.

"Got it. So, I should be able to pull this video from the originating host, and any other place the host sent it to. As of now, that video is a distant memory. The only way it will come up again is if they have it on a hard drive. I've set it so if that ever happens and the hard drive is turned on, it will be deleted automatically. The next time somebody tries you like that, you come tell us what's going on. We could have eliminated your problem the day she came to you with that shit. Hell, you could have talked to Kaleb, and he probably could have cleared it. Or betta yet, his damn mama." Ju pointed at Remi.

I was so relieved. I felt like a weight was lifted off of my shoulders, and I pray that shit never resurfaces. It was time for me to get to the stadium, so I pulled Remi to the side. "I'll see you after the game. Tonight I'm staying with you and the kids, if that's alright?" I smiled down at her.

"We would love that. Play your heart out, out there today." She kissed my lips, and for the first time in a long ass time, I felt free. I know my problems aren't over, nor are things alright with me and Remi, but we have to start somewhere. At least we both know where we stand. We don't have to rush anything, but I don't plan on leaving them. So we definitely gotta figure some shit out. A couple hours later, we were running out of the tunnel, and the crowd was going wild. I looked in the direction of my family, and they were on their feet. Kaleb and Kamryn were jumping up and down, clapping for their dad, and I just couldn't believe they belonged to me.

We were in the two-minute warning. We were down by three points, and the other team had the ball. "We gotta stop this run!" The defense coach yelled. There was a great deal of missed plays that this team needed to work on. If we can stop this run, I get the ball back, and it'll be up to me to move it down the field.

"Listen up. When we get this ball, Calvin, you gotta be ready for me. I'm throwing long every time to get it down the field. If I don't see anyone open, Nick, I'm running it, and I need you and Scott to protect me." Just as I finished talking, defense stopped the play, and it was our turn. We ran out onto the field, and I knew what I had to do. I threw the ball down the field into the fifty-yard line, and the stadium went wild when Calvin caught it. We hurried, got in position before the clock ran out, and I threw another Hail Mary down the field. Calvin fumbled the ball, and the other team recovered running it back for a touchdown. My heart was shattered, I wanted this win for me, my team, and my family. The game was fuckin' over! This dude fumbled the ball in the most important game of our career! I couldn't believe this shit was happening. I was so fuckin' pissed that I walked off the field and down the tunnel to the locker room.

"What the fuckkkkkkk!" I roared, kicking over the trash can in the locker room. The team came into the locker room, and we listened to the coaches give the speech, but I was so pissed I was ready to go. This was some bullshit! I talked to some of my teammates after I got showered and got dressed. Losing the game was devastating and damn sure was going to take some time getting over. When I walked out, my family was waiting for me with somber looks on their faces. I felt like I let everyone down, especially my babies.

"You played your ass off out there, son. That loss wasn't on you." My dad dapped me up, pulling me in for a hug, and I got that from all of my family.

"Dad, you played good." Kaleb stuck his little fist out to dap me up.

"Yeah, don't drop your head, daddy!" Kammy smiled.

"Ohhhh, baby, are you ok? I'm so sorry y'all lost." Saniya stopped in her tracks when she noticed Remi and the kids. "What the hell is she doing here and why didn't you have me sitting with your family?" She looked around at everybody.

"Meet me at home." I looked at her with a smile, and it seemed that she forgot all about Remi and the kids. Kissing me again, she said her goodbyes to the family.

"I damn sure hope that goodbye comes with some slow singing and flower bringing. You can use Trix's casket since we ain't need it for my girl. Let's get out of here. I need that exotic in my lungs, and it's too many damn police around," Grams fussed.

"I'll see you at the hotel a lil' later if that's alright with you?" I looked over at Remi.

"We would like that." She smiled.

"I got something I need to handle tonight. I will be over in the morning for breakfast." I kissed my mom on the cheek and said my goodbyes to my family. They were ready to party, and I just wasn't in the partying mood. The press was on me heavy about the game tonight and about me finding out about my kids. They were still going in on Remi on social media. I hate that all of this shit had to happen the way it did. But I'm ready to heal and have a healthy friendship or relationship if that's the way things are meant for us. Right now, I got some shit I need to get off my chest, and that shit couldn't wait.

After I fought through the press and traffic to get home, it was a little after eight when I pulled into the driveway, and Saniya's was already home. Walking into the house and heading upstairs, I could hear the music coming from our bedroom. Opening the bedroom door, she was laying on the bed naked with rose petals and candles lit all around the room. "Come, let me make you feel better, baby," she requested over the music.

If this was us on a good day, I would have definitely dove into that shit. One thing Saniya had was some good pussy, but good pussy could never make me fuck with an evil bitch! This bitch was willing to destroy me and my fuckin' legacy!

"Nah, I'm gone need you to get the fuck out of my shit!" Myia, Kari, and another chick walked into the room, and Saniya jumped up. Hell, I was still trying to figure out how the hell they got inside the house.

"Thought you needed a lil reinforcement." Kari shrugged.

"What! Did you forget about the shit I have on you, nigga? Don't fuck with me. You think this a game, huh! That video will be sent to the police in a matter of seconds." She laughed.

"Enlighten me; show me the video again," I urged her,

throwing her purse at her. She searched through her phone, moving her fingers fast as hell trying to find that video. That was confirmation for me as well that my brother did his thing with that.

"Wait...Where the fuck is it?!" She jumped up frantically, 'cause shit is about to get all bad for her.

"Just because you deleted it doesn't mean shit, nigga! I have that video secured!" she spat.

"I'll take my fuckin' chances! Get the fuck outta my shit!" I grabbed her by her arms and she started fighting me. She could fight all she wanted. I pulled her ass out of the bedroom, down the stairs, and out of my fuckin' crib, butt ass naked. Fuck this bitch!

"Wait...Please, baby! I'm sorry! I need my clothes!" She cried. Kari stood beside me with her phone and purse. I took all of her credit cards, keys to the house, and bank cards because this bitch had me fucked up. I threw her purse, keys, and phone out to her ass and slammed my door back. Just to be on the safe side, I called a locksmith to come change my locks tonight.

"This was your decision, but I don't think letting her walk was the best decision. You know I always got your back. If shit gets bad, let me know, and she'll be a distant memory. You have someone that really loves you, and I know you love Remi. We saw it in your eyes during the interview. Stop fighting with her and make lasting memories with her and those beautiful, smart babies of yours. I'm so proud of you and love you to death, baby brother." My sister leaned in to kiss my cheek. I appreciated her and my sister in-law so much. They were ready to go to war for me, and that's love.

"That bitch ain't gone do shit. It's best if she moves on and I'll do the same," I said to Kari. We heard Saniya's car speed out of the driveway, and I felt a sigh of relief. I'm not sure where things will end up with me and Remi. We will take things slow, and if it's meant to be, then it shall be. I made sure my home was secured and packed my bags. Since the season had ended, I plan on going back to New York with my kids for a few weeks. If Saniya knew what was best for her, she would stay the fuck away from me.

Chapter Twenty

REMI

Two Months Later

T hings in my world were going alright. My kids are amazing, happy, and healthy. Cam has been back and forth from Atlanta to New York, and for now, that was working for us. We haven't made anything official with us. We're just taking things slow. I wanted more, but I don't know if he's truly ready right now. This morning we had a conversation about how I was feeling, and he was still on that, 'let's take things slow' shit. So, I took that as he didn't want me, and I got pissed. He's been calling, and I've been ignoring his ass. I know I'm acting a little childish, but I'm a little pissed. I don't know why I thought we could just jump into a relationship, but that's not the case. That's just me trying to rush some shit that didn't need to be rushed.

We were leaving to go on a two-week vacation with Cam for his birthday to St. Croix in a couple of days, and I think we were all excited about that. This would be the first time that we're taking a trip together, just me, him, and our kids. So, I guess my attitude needs to get better before we leave.

I got a lead journalist role for real this time. Cam petty ass called me out on that little white lie I told back then. It was because of him they even offered me the position. I had been trying to reach out to Zori to tell her the good news. She hasn't been to work in almost a month, and I stopped by her place a few times to check on her. I'm not sure what's going on with her, but ever since the interview with Cam, she has been on some crazy shit. She told me she was sick, and I believed her, but Johnathan told me he thinks something else was going on with her. There was a knock at the door, and I knew it was Johnathan because his petty ass refuses to use my doorbell.

"One of these days, you're gonna have to use that damn bell."

"I will when you get one that sounds normal. That shit sound like you about to go through the electric chair." We fell out laughing. Johnathan and I worked out our differences, and I even had a talk with Cam about Johnathan. They both agreed to be cordial to each other for the sake of the kids, and I talked with Kammy and Kaleb to let them know they shouldn't call Johnathan daddy.

"So, you really gon' have another baby by this dude?" Johnathan asked, but the look on his face was something different. I just found out a couple days ago that I'm about eight weeks pregnant. I planned on telling Cam for his birthday. I was so excited about being pregnant when I first found out, but now that we've talked this morning, I don't know how to feel.

"Yes, I'm going to have his baby. Why are you saying it like that?" I asked, resting my hand on my hips, 'cause I felt an attitude coming on. I told Johnathan about it because I was so excited about the news, and I couldn't tell Zori because she's been acting funny.

"Nothing, I just remember you saying you wasn't having no more kids. Something just came up; I will call you later." He walked out of the kitchen without giving me time to respond. We were supposed to be going to lunch, and all of a sudden he had to go. I finished doing what I was doing and walked into my bedroom to get dressed. I had some last minute shopping to do, and I'm going to take my babies to lunch. My phone kept beeping, and that let me know I have a text message. I saw it was a voice message from Cam.

It's him for me: Listen, by the time I get to New York. I'mma need you to lose that attitude. We're not doing any of that shit, Rem. Love takes time, and I just wanna take my time with you. You know where I am with this; this shit with you and me is forever. I'm locked in with you, lil mama, and I love you. Hearing him say that had tears flowing down my face, and I immediately dialed his number.

"I want to do everything right with you, beautiful. I wanna take walks in the park, go out on date nights, have baecations, and pour love in and out of you until your fuckin' heart is full. Stop rushing what I have for you' cause this shit with us is on lock." His voice was so deep and sexy, and all I wanted to do right now was crawl in his lap and slide down on his dick.

"Ok!" I cried, and he burst into laughter.

"Ok. I just gave you some raw shit, and all my lil' baby could spit back was ok? I'mma start keeping my deep energy shit to myself." He laughed.

"I'm sorry. I love you too, baby, and if you were here, I would ride your dick right now." I knew he couldn't see me, but the smile was evident in my voice.

"Geeshhh! I'll see you in a few hours, and I want you to ride that muthafucka until you cream yourself to sleep." My damn pussy jumped when he said that. I spoke with Cam a little while longer and then got the kids so that we could head out. Walking downstairs, I saw our security guy in his truck. I got the kids situated in my car and then got in so that we could get our day started. Cam was alright with me driving my car and security following me. We only had one security guard because I felt like one was enough. By the time we got to the mall, it was a little after two, and it was packed in here. I wanted to get the things I needed and get out.

"Mommy, can we get pizza and ice cream?" Kaleb asked, and I know his boss (His sister) put him up to asking me that. Once we were done shopping, I got our food to go, and we headed back to the parking garage, loaded the car up, and headed home. Pulling into my parking garage and getting out, I realized I had a lot of shit. I got the kids out of the car and thank God the guard was with us because he had to help me tote these damn bags. I bought so much stuff that both of our hands were full.

Just as we turned to head to the door, a gunshot went off. I heard my kids screaming, and I was being hit in the face and body over and over again. My kids' cries were excruciating. I tried to fight whoever it was hitting me, but the blows were just too powerful for me. I tried to open my eyes, and everything just went black.

Chapter Twenty-One

SANIYA

I hope Cam and his bitch didn't think I was gone just let them live after what the fuck he did to me. When I said I'm coming for everything, that's what the fuck I meant. I don't know how the fuck he got that video to delete off everything, but he did, and that shit had me ready to fuck everybody up. But I knew I had to plan this shit right!

"Get them into the room!" I yelled, pushing these lil' crying ass punks into the house. The way that nigga did me was fucked up, and I'm gonna make sure that when I kill his stupid, punk ass kids. That will bring that nigga to his knees.

"Why are we here in the hood in this damn house? I thought you were going to get a more secluded place?" Zori questioned me like her ass was running the show.

"Just do what the fuck I say, and this shit will go like we need it to go," I snapped.

"All I know is I want that nigga dead, and my million in my

hands by the end of the fucking night. I really don't give a fuck you do with that fuck nigga kids. I beat the shit outta her ass, so I know that baby she pregnant with is dead!" Johnathan shrugged.

"Auntie Zori and God daddy don't hurt my mommy. She didn't mean to make you upset. Just talk to her, and she will love you, ok?!!" Kammy cried. Zori punched the shit out of the little girl, and she screamed out, crying from the pain.

"Noooo, don't touch my sister!" Kaleb ran to help his sister with tears in his eyes, and just as Zori was about to kick him in his back. I stopped her.

"Well damn! Y'all really got some pent-up aggression against these kids."

"Get them upstairs; let them watch movies with this." I pulled my IPAD out, and Zori and Johnathan laughed.

"I see you've never dealt with your step kids, huh? Meet Doogie Houser. Give this lil' nigga an IPAD if you want too. The cops will be at this door in 2.5 seconds. He can make calls on an IPAD. I got an old laptop in the car. They can watch movies on that," Johnathan said, leaving out to go get the laptop. Zori was standing there in her feelings, and I guess I needed to calm her down because I needed her on top of her game.

"I promise when this is all said and done, you will never have to work another day in your life. All I need you to do is be the beautiful down ass bitch you are. Tonight, I'm going to lick on that pussy extra good." I hungrily attacked her lips and gripped her pussy through her jeans, and she let out a moan. The little girl crying reminded me that they were still in the room. I looked over at them, and the little girl's face was bloody, and her brother was trying to wipe it with his shirt. If I didn't hate they ass so much, I would've thought him looking out for her was some admirable shit. Johnathan walked back into the house with the laptop, and we got the kids upstairs and situated.

"Can I play a game?" Kaleb asked, and Johnathan looked at me.

"Why the hell you looking at me? Open it up and let his ass play the game. I'm going to fuck on my girl. Go get them some food or something. When we're done, we will figure out how we gonna get this money. We're not making a move until I say so," I told him as we turned to look at Kaleb because his little fingers were moving on that laptop. I moved over to him and snatched the computer to see what the fuck he was doing.

"What the fuck are all these numbers, letters, and symbols for. What kind of game is this?" I looked down at him, and his little innocent face almost got me.

"It's Minecraft game, see." He stood up to show me the game. I threw the laptop back on the bed, and he got back on the bed next to his sister. I walked out of the room and into the bedroom, me and Zori were going to be sleeping in. She was in the shower when I walked into the bathroom.

"Stop being like that with me, babe." I removed my clothes as I watched her slide her fingers in and out of her pussy. Stepping into the shower, I replaced her fingers with mine and moved in and out of her. I placed light kisses on her lips, trailing kisses down to her breasts. Her tongue grazed my nipple as her fingers massaged my clit, a moan escaped my lips and that was it for me she had me ready to strap my shit on and fuck the shit out of her.

"I need you!" she cried out, gripping my titty with one hand as she slid her fingers inside of my wet pussy. I was losing it. If she didn't know how to do anything else, baby girl knew how to make me feel good.

"Fuck! This some wet ass pussy. You know I'mma tear this

pussy up!" I stepped out of the shower, pulling her behind me. We crawled in the bed, and the moment she spread her legs, I dove in, sucking the shit out of that pussy. I had my baby screaming. In minutes she was bustin' so damn hard. I stood up, put my strap on, and tore that pussy up for hours. My girl needed some attention, so I decided to give her that for a little while.

Chapter Twenty-Two

CAM

"I don't give a fuck who we have to go through to get to these niggas! They touched my girl and got my fuckin' kids! They touched my kids, dad! They can come for me all day, but I will gladly do life behind bars for my kids and my girl! Fuck football, fuck my image. Until my kids are safely back with their mother, all that other shit is out the window!" I roared, pulling both of my guns out and tucking them in my back.

"Yo, it made the news!" Truth pointed to the television.

"That's that shit I hate. Shit like this; we don't need to be made public. We don't need no damn help from the cops!" Uncle Zelan was pissed just like the rest of us.

Remi was bruised up pretty bad, but she was going to be alright. Right now, the baby is fine, but she was still early in her pregnancy, so the doctors said we need to watch her for the next forty-eight hours. We're both staying here with my parents until we find out who snatched our kids. The guard that was with them was killed, and I'm wondering why they didn't hurt Remi any worse than they did. It was almost as if they didn't want to hurt her.

"I can't believe this shit!" Kari was about to explode

"Boss lady, what do you need us to do?" One of the girls asked her.

"Cam, are you alright?" Kari wrapped her arms around me, and I just held onto my sister.

"Yooo, what the fuck is that!" Uncle Z pointed at the television, and that shit got all of our attention. It turned black and it read Love Is Love with a bunch of numbers, letters, and symbols on it. Love is Love? I used to say that to Remi all the time back in college.

"Is something going on with the T.V down there?" Grams asked through the intercom.

"Yeah," Kari responded to her, just as it started blinking the words and numbers across the screen.

"What in the Poltergeist vs. Poltergeist shit is this? Ion do ghosts. That's some new-new shit right there. Ion even think my blow torch can burn ghost. Truth, I think we should bow out and let these niggas figure this shit out on they own. Cause going up against niggas that float in the air just ain't some shit we should get into." Uncle Gabe ass was going on and on.

"Cam! It's Kaleb! It's Kaleb! I'm coming down." We heard Remi cry out through the intercom. Just as I was about to take off for the elevator, Kari stopped me. "I'll go get her."

"I need my laptop! I think the numbers are codes." JuJu said and ran out of the room. A few minutes later, Ju, Remi, and Kari came back into the room.

"Cameron, that's our baby, I taught him, and Kamryn Love Is Love as a safe word for help!" She cried. My heart hurt because I had no fuckin' clue how I was going to get my babies back, but I would die trying and that's a fact.

"Ummm how can it be a safe word if they need help? I'm so confused. Maybe if I get high that will help my confusion." Uncle Gabe shook his head.

"Nigga, shut yo' ass up," Uncle Zelan told him. The code flashed on the screen again, and my brother's fingers were moving so damn fast you barely see them on the keys.

"Fuckkkk! I can't get it!" Ju spat.

"Do you have another computer?" Remi asked him, and I helped her over to the bar where JuJu was sitting. He opened his other laptop, Remi pulled her glasses out of her pocket and put them on. In that moment I fell in love all over again. It was my Remi the woman I fell in love with back in college. The woman that birthed my children, and the woman that was carrying my seed now.

"JuJu, there is something blocking the last part of the code. If we can get passed, that we can get his encrypted message. Dammit!" Remi shouted.

"What's going on? Why the fuck does your Ex, and Remi's friends have my grandchildren! Somebody better start talking and talk right the hell now!" My dad roared, and I told him everything.

"What the fuck were you thinking!" He looked at me with disappointment on his face.

"I was young and not thinking at all, dad. I'm sorry, but i can't worry about that now. Please help me get my kids." I pleaded with him.

"Ju, how did Kaleb know to alert us here at the house?" My dad asked.

"He must have sent it to the User ID and passwords he could

remember. Kaleb's code is an encrypted message. He locked it down so good you have to break it out in pieces. I can't believe this shit; this kid is five years old! The good thing about it is we know he sent it and that tells us that they're safe." Ju and Rem were still going at it.

"Damn! When we get them back, all my money going into whatever lil' nephew wanna get into! 'Cause if he got his genius ass uncle stuck that lil nigga the one!" Uncle Zelan stated.

"And that's on JESUS!" Uncle Gabe blurted, but that shit was funny.

I got it!" JuJu yelled out. And the entire message appeared on the television and his computer. It said that *Saniya, Zori, and God daddy Johnathan have us. I don't know the exact address but attached is the coordinates. They hurt my sister, please help us.*

"Nooooooooo! My babies!" Remi screamed out.

"Urrgghhhhhh! These bitch niggas are going to die!" I roared.

"Oh my God! Juelz, get my grandbabies! I want them out of there right now! Juelzzzz, get them now!" My mother cried out as she held onto my dad.

"Ain't the Zori chick and Johnathan dude your so-called friends?" Kari asked Remi.

"Yeah, and I never would have thought they would want to hurt my children?" she cried.

"Let's go! Ju, you can work in the car, or stay here and talk to us by phone." My dad was talking as he walked out the door. All the men in the room followed him out, and when we got outside, the Diamond Clique was getting out of their trucks.

"Ahhhhhh hell, my girls coming to ride one last time! Them some bad bitches right there!" Grams was standing on the steps, clapping her hands.

"Ma, since it's our last ride, you might as well join us," he said to my Grams, and this damn lady ran in the house and came back out with this duffle bag.

"Ma, I'm telling you now yo' old ass betta not pass the hell out or try no ole slick shit. The things you used to do back in the day, yo' old ass can't do no mo'!" Uncle Gabe had everybody laughing.

"Nigga, I done told y'all the only thing old is the paper they printed my certificate a birth on," she fussed.

"Yo' ass so old, they probably done discontinued them guns you think you 'bout to bust! The grenades ain't gone blow shit up but dust," Uncle Gabe told her, and we all fell out laughing.

"I got the address! Let's go!" Ju ran out of the house and jumped into dad's truck. I have never seen any of them in action, but I guess I was about to see what it was all about with them. Uncle Gabe walked up to the truck and opened the door, looking in.

"Where I'm supposed to sit at?" He asked.

"We don't have room. Umm, go ride with the girls. They would love to have you ride with them one more time!" Uncle Truth laughed.

"What girls!" He started looking all around. "Cause nigga I know you fuckin lyin', if you think I'm getting in the car with them extra aggressive, kill a nigga for cutting his eye at them, heavy-handed, blade throwing, slice your neck while you at the gas station, paralyze you from the neck down, stare at you like you stank, Diamond Clique! Hell to the nawl! JuJu, get yo' ass out and go ride with your wife and her crew." Uncle Gabe had us in this truck bent over in laughter.

"Nah, I feel safer with my dad! I did it for you the last time, and I felt uncomfortable. You on your own now." Ju shrugged, and even Dad fell out laughing.

"I'm about to tell them you over here talking about them and called they mamas ugly!" Uncle Gabe ass was petty 'cause he was walking fast as hell to the other trucks.

We pulled on the block in Harlem of the address Ju gave us. A few minutes later, Uncle Meek and Uncle Gabe walked up to the truck.

"What's the plan?" he asked, and if that's the house my kids are in, then fuck a plan. I got out of the car, pulling both of my guns out, moving towards the house.

"Cam!" I heard my dad yell out. Kari ran up to catch up with me, and before I knew it, her crew was climbing the house like they were damn Spiderman. *What the fuck!*

"These heifers just ain't natural. Like how can they see, she don't even have a flashlight? I know they on our team, but they ass just makes me nervous. I'm supposed to feel comfortable with my teammates. I be confused and praying they don't turn and shoot me because I twitched or sum shit." I shook my head at Uncle Gabe and kicked the door in! my kids were inside, and I needed to get to them.

"This nigga need to stick to football 'cause this ain't it. Leave the killing to us! We rides down on 'em; so they never see us coming." Grams had her choppa out and this nigga Johnathan came running downstairs with his gun blasting, and Grams, Meek, and Truth lit his ass up.

"Yesssuhhhh! Y'all betta let 'em know ain't shit old 'bout Lai but these muthafuckin' bullets baby. Chile, y'all kill the rest of they ass. I need my asthma pump." She fanned us off. Meek and Truth started up the steps and was stopped in their tracks when Zori had Kaleb with her gun pointed to his head! And Saniya had my screaming baby girl hanging over the banister by just her shirt. If she let her go, the drop had to be every bit of fifteen to twenty feet. This was a three-story level house. My heart dropped and my soul left my body.

"Get the fuck back! I will kill these lil' bastards! Y'all gone back the fuck up and let me and my girl walk the fuck up out of here!" Saniya yelled and I have never in my life wanted a bitch dead as bad as I wanted her ass dead!

"Girl, what the fuck!" I was confused as fuck.

Nigga, Zori has been my girl for years, since college to be exact. I knew everything about your bitch, and her kids. I knew she was pregnant by you, the moment she found out. I wanted you for myself, I wanted the fame, I wanted the money, and I wanted your bitch ass to love me because I really loved you. The dick was amazing, and I'm damn sure gone miss that shit, but fuck you! I knew you loved her, I heard you call her name in your sleep many of nights. I knew if you found out that she was pregnant, and the baby was yours you would've left me. I wasn't having that shit; I had a lifestyle that I wanted to live, and you were going to give it to me. That bitch Remi has always been in the fuckin way! That video was my meal ticket, and I knew I could get your ass to do whatever I needed you to do to save your ass. I just wasn't prepared for your geek ass brother to make the shit vanish. Zori and I had plans, and you fucked all of that up. Zori has never been a friend to that bitch, it was team Saniya from the beginning. Now this dead stupid nigga Johnathan, well he was just pissed because Remi kept choosing you. He wanted her for himself, and she would never go against you for him. We

149

just fed him some bullshit, and he was down to help get rid of your ass.

"All that I knew you were full of shit, bitch! I knew it was more to it than just the money, you really wanted to be with this nigga. I can't believe I fell for your bullshit, all these years. You were right about one thing, I purposely made sure that Remi came to that interview. Even though I couldn't stand the bitch, I knew deep down how much she loved his ass, and we knew he loved her." Zori cried.

"Zo, calm down, don't do this shit now. Let me get us out of here baby and I promise it's going to be just me and you." Saniya tried to convince her.

"You bitches not walking out of here alive! When I kill you, I promise you'll never see that shit coming," Kari told her just as Myia carefully made herself visible to us, standing behind Saniya.

"Bitch, fuck you! I never liked you, your ghetto ass grand-mother, or your bougie bitch of a mother," Saniya spat.

"Oh, hell to the nawl! Slit that bitch from the rootah to the muthafuckin' tootah!" Grams yelled. My eyes went from my son to my daughter and they both were screaming their little hearts out.

"Juelz, we got the stairs. All your focus should be on the banister," Uncle Truth said to him.

"Kaleb, stop crying, son. Daddy's here, and I promise I won't let anything happen to you." I looked him in his eyes, and he calmed down.

"How are you going to stop it, nigga?!" Zori questioned, and I couldn't believe this bitch was in on this shit. Kaleb bit her leg, and she screamed out, getting temporarily distracted. Uncle

Meek took the shot, hitting her in the head and Kaleb ran down the stairs.

"Nooooooooo!" Saniya screamed. She let go of my daughter, and I moved quick, trying to catch her because if she hit the bottom, it would kill her. Kari eased up the stairs, and her and Myia opened fire on Saniya. I caught Kammy and crashed to the floor, but the way I caught her may have caused some injuries to us both.

"You alright, son?" He questioned as he pulled my screaming, bloody daughter from my arms, trying to calm her. It broke my heart to hear her tell him she hurts all over and to see my dad wipe the tears from his eyes. It killed me because how bad was my baby hurt.

"We gotta get them to the hospital, and we need to get a clean-up crew here!" My dad moved out of the house with Kammy in his arms, and Uncle Meek had Kaleb. Uncle Zelan, Ju, and Uncle Gabe helped me out of the house. It took about twenty minutes to get us to the emergency room. An hour later, Remi and my mom came running into the room. Kaleb was fine, but Kammy and I both had broken arms, and she had some bruises on her face. The way I fell to the floor, I injured my back, but overall, we were going to make it. My dad and Jeff dealt with the cops, and Raheim gave a statement to the press by phone. God really stepped in and saved my girl, and my babies and I'm forever grateful.

Chapter Twenty-Three

❧

REMI

One Year Later

"Mmmm, fuck me, baby!" I begged out as he stroked me so good. We had been going at it all damn day, and I don't think his ass was going to stop anytime soon.

"Damn! I can't get enough of this good ass pussy!" He pounded me over and over again.

"Shit, I'm cumming, baby!" I cried out.

"Let that shit go, lil mama!" I came so hard my body started to shake. Every time I cum, this nigga has my body shaking like I'm having a seizure.

"Ohhhh fuck!" he growled, and we both released together. After we gathered our composure, we got up to take a shower so that we could go have some dinner. Cam and I were doing amazingly well, and the kids were so excited to have us all under the same roof. He had a house built for us, and we moved down to

Atlanta to be with him. Juelz Sr. even sent contractors to our new home and had an ice cream parlor built on our property. He just signed a three year, two hundred million dollar deal to stay in Atlanta. He became a free agent after winning the Superbowl this time around, and that caused his price tag to go through the roof. They came back this year with something to prove, and that is all Kammy talks about is her daddy being a Super bowl champ.

I still couldn't believe the two people I trusted the most were the two that never even gave a fuck about me. Because of Zori and Johnathan, I don't want new friendships, and Cam says he doesn't want me to feel that way. If it's not my man, kids, and immediate family, I don't want it. I gave birth to another beautiful daughter, Autumn Renee. We love everything about that little girl, and she looks just like Kammy. Kammy and Kaleb healed from the incident, but Kammy is still battling with nightmares of it all. Even though the incident happened a year ago, I wanted to make sure my children got the help they needed. So, we decided to put them in counseling. Today was Cam's birthday, and we were in St. Lucia on a Baecation. The kids were in New York with their grandparents, and they were having the time of their lives. Kammy called excited because her Papa owned his own plane. She talked him into taking her to the American Doll store in Manhatten. Juelz worked it out with a nearby hotel that had a helipad, and he used his helicopter that's on the property to take his granddaughter, and grandson to go toy shopping. Ciera, and Juelz has these kids definitely spoiled. I was loving every moment of my freedom. We were having a candlelight dinner on the beach.

"You know to be honest with you, the day I met you I knew it was something special about you. The more time I spent with you, the more my heartbeat for you. I used to think I was so stupid and was afraid to tell you how I felt. My fear was always what people would think of me for dating the little geeky girl on campus, and that was the dumbest shit ever.

I've always felt incomplete, and you were the one that I needed. You complete me, baby. On some real shit, you were always that missing piece for me. My life will never work without you and my children. Thank you for being you. You're everything I prayed for in this lifetime. I love you from the pit of my soul, baby." He stood pulling me out of my seat, and we both were in tears.

This man was everything to me, and I was so happy that we made the decision to get married here on this island. We decided that we wanted to do this alone and later do something with our family. It wasn't planned. We just decided to call the hotel earlier today and asked how we could get married. They handled everything we needed and suggested a jeweler on the island for us. Right before we had our dinner, Cam and I got married, and it was the most beautiful ceremony I've ever witnessed. I cried, he cried, and most importantly, we vowed to love one another forever!

"You know it's not going anywhere, right?" Cam laughed at me, because I was admiring the ten karat princess cut diamond on my finger.

"I know; I just can't help it. I'm so happy! Do you think everyone will be mad about what we did?"

"I really don't care; we didn't do this to hurt anyone's feelings. This was something that we wanted to do for us, Mrs. Kassom. You can't worry about what other people think. You wanted to get married, I wanted to get married, and we did that shit. Now hurry up and eat that lobster, so I can eat you." He laughed.

"That shit sounded corny, huh?" We both fell out laughing. After dinner, we went back to our suite, and for the rest of the night, we consummated our marriage. Life was good. I married the man that I've longed for, and God has blessed us tremendously.

The end!

Made in the USA
Las Vegas, NV
20 May 2022

49151410R00095